CHASING RABBITS

RODOLFO DEL TORO

ISBN 978-1-7337819-4-7

For Janice, Natalia and Daniela

*"Let's make the most of the time,
because wasting time is the most expensive thing of all"*

Vincent Van Gogh

CHAPTER 1

PRESENT DAY.

Having finished earlier than expected with his last patient, an easy post-op visit, Rudy spent the next few minutes on his computer checking the status of a few online orders. Glancing at the clock on the bottom right-hand corner of the computer monitor, he got up and walked over to the adjacent exam room. Inside, he expected to find his next patient, but to his surprise, Rudy walked into an empty room. Puzzled, Rudy checked the next exam room and found it to be empty as well.

"Luz!" Rudy called. "What happened to the afternoon appointments?"

"Don't know. I confirmed them yesterday and again this morning. We didn't have any cancellations; they just didn't show. Shall I send them bills as no-shows?" Luz asked.

"Nah, it's Friday. It's a long weekend. Let's consider it an early dismissal. We can get out of the city early and beat the rush," Rudy replied.

Luz became excited, as she had the longest commute, which without exception turned murderous on Fridays. Luz then seemed to remember something, reaching for a small envelope on her desk, which she offered to Rudy.

"Sorry, Doc. This was hand delivered this morning. I know you don't like to get mail on Fridays, but it doesn't look like bad news," she turned the envelope over before she handed it to Rudy. "It looks like an invitation. The man who delivered it looked like a butler."

Rudy hated going to the post office and checking mail on Fridays. If it was bad news like a notice from the IRS, a new exciting way for insurance companies to screw him over, or anything that would spoil his weekend, there was nothing he could do about it. He would have to wait until Monday, so he avoided checking mail on Fridays. With a reluctant sigh, Rudy accepted the envelope, giving Luz a mild look of disapproval.

"The address is local, from someone named M. Davenport!" she added.

For a second, Rudy felt as if the wind had been knocked out of him. He slowly fell into a chair in complete disbelief. His complexion must have shown it, as an alarmed Luz jumped up from her chair and moved to his side.

"Are you okay? It's bad news, isn't it? I knew I should have waited until Tuesday," she said with guilt in her voice.

"No, no, it's okay. I don't think its bad news. It's just that's a name I haven't heard in a long time," Rudy said, his mind racing into the past. "A long time."

"So you know him? I don't remember you ever talking about him. It *is* a him, right?" Luz said, both reprimanding and cautioning Rudy.

"Yes!" Rudy couldn't help but chuckle at the implication.

Luz always looked out for Rudy. She had been his secretary since his return to the West Coast eight years ago and acted as a surrogate mother. She was always in his corner, covering for him whenever he needed it. More than one electric guitar had been mailed to her house in secret. She had even kept an old car at her house until Rudy worked up the courage to tell his wife he bought it. When he got divorced, Luz and her husband helped him through that difficult time, becoming his extended family. In fact, Luz knew almost everything about his life, but not about his friendship with Mike, or what they went through that last year of medical school. Rudy had never told her about this. In fact, he had not spoken of it, nor seen or heard from Mike, since it happened.

"Well, who is he?" Luz asked insistently.

"My God, could it really be Mike?" Rudy asked out loud.

"Mike?" Luz asked.

"Mortimer Davenport the Second. He was named after his grandfather. He really hated being called that," Rudy explained as he unconsciously looked at the envelope and felt all those years wash away. He fell into a silent trance until Luz brought him back.

"So?"

"He was a friend from med school. At first I really didn't get along with Mike; none of us did. See, med school is like high school, except the divisions between the groups are a bit blurred and the groups tend to merge over time. It boils down to competition, but most people get along. Not Mike. He was disliked from day one. For one thing, he was wealthy. There were other wealthy students, but not like Mike. He was obscenely wealthy; his father was worth billions."

"That's no reason to dislike him," Luz said.

"True, but his father made his money on the insurance market, and at the time he was homing in on medical insurance, strangling hospitals and almost every doctor in the state in the process. Since most of our teachers and more than a few of the students' parents were doctors, they were feeling the strain from Mike's father. Of course, that didn't make him popular. He was also kind of a loner; he didn't hang out with anyone or attend our parties. If we happened to run into him while hanging out, he would acknowledge us, of course, but never join us. We would always see him with models, occasionally with celebrities, and always driving extravagant cars."

"You aren't like that. How did you get to be friends?" Luz asked, frowning.

"Not easily, not at first. It was because of our last names; his is Davenport, I'm Dell. We were always assigned together at lab tables. Whenever the class was broken down into groups, we would end up together. Since most people didn't want anything to do with him, I ended up paired with him almost exclusively. It turned out he wasn't a jerk; he just kept his distance because he knew people in the medical community despised his father."

"Was he like his father, only after money?" Luz asked.

"No, although I thought as much in the beginning. I really believed he was just after the title so he could work for his father and use the 'MD' to justify the decisions his father's company made," Rudy said.

"He wasn't?" Luz asked.

"No; at least, he didn't seem to be. During our rotations and clerkships together, he really cared about the patients. Not at all what you would expect from the son of Rupert Davenport," Rudy said.

"So what happened? Something had to happen to get you so worked up," Luz said.

Rudy nodded silently.

"By our fourth year, we were good friends. We even planned our clerkships together. He somehow managed to get me to do a full month of trauma surgery in New York. It was a nightmare," Rudy said.

"That bad?" Luz said.

"It did seal my resolve that I was not going to be a trauma surgeon," Rudy said, nodding.

"And?"

"We came back a little over two weeks before Christmas. We had scheduled a nice clerkship at the outpatient dermatology clinics. Since it was close to the holidays, the clinics wouldn't run at full capacity, and we wouldn't have call duty. Not to mention that we would have been free from before Christmas day and up to and past New Year's. Time to study for the boards," Rudy said.

Luz raised an eyebrow inquisitively. "You sacrificed a holiday?"

"I was different back then. Very competitive. Only grades and standing meant anything. I was a moron," Rudy took a solemn breath of remembrance before continuing. "When we got to dermatology, we found our clerkship had been canceled and were sent back to the med school. There we found out our schedules had been changed and we were sent to the pediatric ER, but we ended up in oncology. That's when it all began," Rudy said, startled when he felt his throat catch with the words.

"I didn't mean to pry. You don't have to talk about it if it's difficult," said Luz in a concerned tone.

"No, it's okay. About time I tell someone. Who better?" Rudy said, and he meant it.

Involuntarily, Rudy found himself about to tell a story he hadn't told anyone, a story he had never planned on telling, but Luz was family. He wondered if he was strong enough to go back to that place, that time in late December 1995.

CHAPTER 2

DECEMBER 1995

"I'm sorry about this," said Mike.

"It's not your fault. They do stuff like this all the time," Rudy replied.

"No, not this time. I'm being punished and I'm taking you down with me," replied Mike.

Rudy couldn't see why. It wasn't the first time one of his clerkships changed. He wasn't too happy about it, but he didn't understand why Mike thought this was his fault. As if reading his confusion, Mike turned, frowning for an instant.

"Extended Health," Mike managed to say before he continued walking.

"Your father's company?" Rudy asked.

Mike nodded and inhaled deeply before continuing. "They just implemented some new policies that are making things more difficult for doctors and facilities."

"So you think this is payback?" Rudy asked.

"It is."

Could it really be? Rudy wondered. Their original schedule had them doing three weeks of outpatient dermatology clinics. Since it was December, the clinics would be running with skeleton crews and thus would have very few patients, which meant very little work. Not only that, but two fourth-year medical students, neither of whom were remotely interested in dermatology, would constitute a hindrance to the residents. That would create a window of opportunity, or at the very least the distinct possibility of being dismissed early each day. Instead they were now headed to the children's hospital for three weeks of emergency room pediatrics.

***

Mike and Rudy had indeed arrived early at the dermatology clinics. There they were surprised by the news that they were not scheduled for a clerkship, and were told to report back to the medical school for reassignment. Once there, no one seemed to know what was going on. So they spent the better part of the day moving back and forth between offices. After bouncing around, they found themselves at the dean's office. There they finally learned what was to be their new assignment. By this time they were already late, and far from the hospital.

Getting to the children's hospital took longer than expected. It was not only quite a drive, but the late afternoon traffic was more than they expected. Thus it was almost four o'clock when they finally made it to the hospital.

"Well, buddy, could be worse," Rudy said.

"Really? How so?" asked Mike.

"We could be stuck with Sister Ann for the next few weeks," Rudy said as he smirked.

Mike came to an abrupt halt as he heard the name of his classmate. He rolled his eyes while shaking his head.

"No, please no, kill me. At least she hates you more than she hates me."

"Nothing like having a fellow student to assure me that I'm going to hell. Repeatedly," Rudy said, nodding in affirmation.

"What did you do to her?" Mike asked.

"Nothing," Rudy replied, smiling.

Mike frowned.

"I was late to a Saturday study session and I was wearing an AC/DC shirt. She saw it, and pointing at it, she said I was going to hell. So I asked her if she was going to heaven. She nodded, all smug. So I told her I'd rather go to hell and not have to deal with her."

Mike nodded as he laughed loudly.

***

Walking past the main doors to the children's hospital, they hurried down the long corridor leading to the emergency room. Once there, Mike and Rudy became engulfed by sounds and furious motion. Doctors, nurses, and all sorts of staff rushed in all directions. Around them, the monitors beeped loudly, their sound melding with the voices of children of all ages who spoke, yelled, or cried. When the staff's conversations were added to the mix, it all formed a disturbing cacophony. Dodging the fast-moving staff, the duo made their way to the nurses' station, where they had been told to meet Dr. Zamberg, the attending physician in charge of the emergency room.

As they moved in, Rudy looked down at the long main nurses' station. At the far corner, a group of doctors stood around a bright view-box illuminator. The huddled group consisted of six individuals who all wore white coats, two of them short. Rudy knew those two were medical students, just like him. All of them remained transfixed by the bright images in front of them. None spoke.

"Excuse me, we are looking for Dr. Zamberg," Rudy said as he walked closer to the doctors.

A female doctor turned slowly. Her demeanor conveyed frank annoyance.

"And you are?" the doctor asked.

"We are the two medical students assigned to the emergency room for the next three weeks," Rudy said as he read her name tag.

Zamberg looked them over, her expression strange. She didn't seem to be confused, but rather hesitant.

"What's your name?" Zamberg asked as she pointed at Rudy.

"Rudy Dell."

"I'm Mike Davenport," volunteered Mike.

Zamberg glared at Mike.

"I know who you are," Zamberg replied in a despondent tone. She then turned back to Rudy, hesitating for an instant as if to say something. Zamberg shook her head and returned to the CT scan.

"You have been reassigned. Go to oncology and find Doctor Betances," Zamberg said as she continued to stare at the CT scan.

"She has a right orbital floor fracture," Rudy said, surprising everyone, especially himself.

"Show me. How do you know it's a she?" Zamberg asked, clearly surprised.

Rudy moved closer and pointed to one of the views.

"See here, and here, it's not that big, and here. From what I can see in these other views, there isn't any displacement or muscle entrapment," Rudy then pointed to the uppermost corner of the scan. "Her name is Lisa. I'm pretty sure that's not a boy's name. What happened, baseball?"

"Softball," Zamberg replied in an amused tone. She turned and glared at the residents around her before turning back to Rudy, who realized he had just upstaged Zamberg's residents and students.

"Dell, where are you going next year?" she asked.

"Surgery."

"Interested in pediatric surgery?" Zamberg asked.

"Plastics, actually."

Zamberg nodded.

"You'll do well. Promise to be kind and take care of any children with cleft palates that come your way," Zamberg said.

"I volunteer with Doctor Chen in his charity plastic clinic," Rudy said proudly.

"Do you?" Zamberg said, raising an eyebrow. Rudy got the distinct impression she was reading him. "Are you eager to help, or are you just working on improving your CV?"

Rudy felt a chill as he realized that Zamberg had read him. He considered protesting but thought better of it. Anyone who could read him so clearly would make a quick meal of any bullshit excuse he came up with. He was wondering how she managed to see through him so easily when she addressed him.

"You could have learned a lot here, but the decision has been made. It's out of my hands. Sixth floor, oncology, find Doctor Betances."

Cursing under his breath, Rudy boarded the elevator. Mike followed close behind.

"Have you heard about Betances?" asked Mike.

Rudy shook his head. He really hadn't but was struck by Mike's worried expression.

"I have," Mike said.

"And?" Rudy asked as the elevator doors opened on the fifth floor.

"He's former military, some kind of special forces. They say that when he was a resident, he had this one patient. Parental abuse, battered child, and the dad didn't even deny it. So he grabbed the dad by the neck and raised him off the floor, choking him until the nurses managed to calm him down," Mike said, trepidation in his voice.

"Very Darth Vader of him. No one can do that. Regardless, he would have been dismissed and charged with assault. The guy would have sued him. He would have never finished his residency. That's just an urban myth," Rudy said as the elevator doors closed and the elevator continued its trip up.

A moment later, the doors opened on the sixth floor, where to their dismay, their fellow student Ana Walton waited for them.

"This is your fault, Davenport," Walton said.

"Take it easy, sister. He hasn't done anything," Rudy exclaimed.

Mike exhaled and was trying to reassure Rudy when Walton exploded.

"Do not call me that. And it *is* Davenport's fault. Zamberg told me as much; something about his father. I have no interest in dermatology, and now thanks to you two that's where I'm headed," Walton explained in a loud voice.

"What the hell is going on?" a deep voice growled from around a corner.

The nurse who had been writing at the station next to them closed the chart she was working on. She got up and gathered her things. Giving them a sorry look that Rudy could have sworn was that of pity for the condemned, she walked away.

In an instant, a man came around the corner, wearing a well-worn but impeccable white lab coat. The tower of a man walked up and stood in front of them.

"Doctor Betances," Walton managed before he raised a finger to silence her.

Rudy stared at Betances. Unlike so many of his attendings, the man was clearly physically strong; in fact, he was robust. He wore an angry but controlled expression on his burly face. Moving past Walton and Rudy without giving them but a passing glance, Betances moved straight towards Mike. Rudy recalled what Mike had said about Betances—how he had choked a man—which at the time Rudy had dismissed as utter nonsense. Upon seeing Betances's physical appearance and menacing demeanor, Rudy reconsidered. He was now quite sure Betances was more than capable of both lifting and choking someone. In fact, judging by his expression, Rudy feared Betances seemed intent on proving this with Mike.

Walking within inches of Mike, Betances stared angrily at him. Mike was a bit taller than Betances, but it made no difference. Mike seemed to shrink. Not to mention that Betances's shoulders were so broad that Mike all but disappeared behind him.

"Watson, what are you still doing here? You have been reassigned to dermatology. If I have to repeat myself you'll never set foot in this hospital again," Betances said in a low growl. "Dell, you are free to leave with Watson. Doctor Davenport will be staying with us," Betances added in a calm but sentencing tone.

The elevator doors opened as if on cue. Watson quickly moved inside, but Rudy didn't. He stayed behind.

"Dell!" Watson insisted.

After looking at her blankly, Rudy turned to Mike, who still stood with his back against the wall as Betances continued to stand inches from him. Mike's ominous expression was that of true fear, and that sealed Rudy's resolve. He would have rather done an easy rotation and gotten some studying done. That would certainly help his class standing. Ultimately, guilt swayed Rudy. He could not bring himself to leave his friend alone, not to mention that the notion of spending three weeks with Sister Ann made him nauseous.

"I'll stay here. Seems like a good opportunity to learn," Rudy said.

Watson frowned. She shook her head and allowed the elevator doors to close. Rudy watched, then turned back to Mike, only to find Betances eyeing him.

"An opportunity to learn? Davenport doesn't deserve your loyalty," Betances said with loathing. He finally backed off. "We just finished afternoon rounds and are about to start call. Dell, go home. Morning rounds start at seven a.m."

Rudy nodded silently. He understood that while Betances would start rounds at seven a.m., he needed to be at the hospital well before that. By the time Betances arrived, Rudy should have checked on every patient, and have every lab result, test, and occurrence noted. It was clear to Rudy he had to be there by six a.m., at least.

"Rudy, call Julia," Mike said.

Momentarily confused, Rudy was going to ask him why, when Betances spoke.

"Davenport, you are on call today. Follow me. I want you to meet your patients," Betances again moved close to Mike. "You know, the ones your father says are a waste of money since most of them are going to die anyway."

Mike's face flushed, then lost most of its color. His eyes darted to Rudy, who could have sworn Mike's eyes expressed a deep shame. Betances seemed to notice this and swiftly turned in Rudy's direction.

"What are you still doing here?" Betances said. His intent was clear. This was an ultimatum.

CHAPTER 3

After the scolding look Rudy got from Betances, he decided not to press his luck and slowly made his retreat. Rudy did not leave the hospital the same way he came in, avoiding the emergency room this time around. Once out of the hospital he turned into the parking lot, there he quickly found his old Jeep. Rudy climbed inside, shivering. Winters in California were mostly mild compared to the rest of the States. But a ragtop Jeep with windows that barely closed soaked up the cold and kept it in, literally becoming an ice cave. The Jeep roared to life after a few turns of the ignition. As soon as it did, Rudy reached for the heater knob and set it to high. Slowly, hot air began blowing around him. Regardless, it took several minutes for the car's interior to become comfortable enough. Rudy reached for the steering wheel and was surprised by how cold it was. Releasing it, he rubbed his hands before gripping it again, then finally drove off.

Rudy drove to his apartment, thinking he could get a few hours of studying done. On the way, he thought about what Mike had told him to do. Why did Mike want him to call Julia? He was a few blocks from his apartment when it finally dawned on him; they had dinner plans with Julia.

Julia was Mike's friend, one of the few Rudy had actually met. From what Rudy could gather, they had known each other since they were kids, so he always assumed she was from his world. An up-and-coming fashion model, she had intimidated

Rudy when he first met her. He had, of course, seen her pictures in fashion ads before. In those photos she was beautiful, but in real life she was actually more than that; she was more so, stunning. She wasn't as tall as Rudy had expected, but tall enough, with perfect cheekbones and facial symmetry. As a future plastic surgeon, Rudy noticed such things. Her expression was what you could call picture-perfect. When she smiled, the room lit up, and her laughter was loud and boisterous. Contrary to what he expected, she was laid-back, fun, and extremely down-to-earth, and genuinely seemed to enjoy spending time with Mike and Rudy.

"You guys are normal. You aren't trying to impress me, you aren't fake, and you don't fidget when I'm around," Julia had told Rudy once when he asked.

Little did she know that she still made Rudy very nervous. After all, she was a celebrity.

Once home, Rudy called Julia, praying he would get her answering machine so he could leave a message and get out of dinner. To his dismay, she answered on the second ring.

"Hello," Julia said cheerfully.

"Hey, Julia. It's Rudy, you know, Mike's friend." Rudy cringed. Of course she knew who he was.

"Rudy . . . Rudy . . . No, doesn't ring a bell," Julia said.

Rudy took a deep breath, unclear as to how to proceed.

"Really, *Mike's friend?* I know who you are, you idiot," Julia added, laughing loudly. "Don't tell me you are calling to cancel."

"Well..." Rudy fidgeted nervously, wondering what the hell was wrong with him. He wasn't nervous around other women; well, not always. He took a deep breath and continued, trying to sound as nonchalant as possible. "Yeah, I'm sorry. We had an unexpected change of schedule. Mike is on call tonight."

"What about you?" Julia asked.

"Me?" Rudy replied.

"Are you on call?" Julia seemed to smirk before she continued, "I'm getting the distinct impression you don't want to go out to dinner with me!"

"No, no. I mean, since Mike can't make it, I—" Rudy managed.

"Perfect. It's settled. Pick us up as planned. Wait, unless Tania makes you uncomfortable. I can tell her dinner is off," Julia said, cutting him off.

Rudy didn't know what to say. Tania? Rudy had no clue who this Tania was. Mike had just told him about the dinner plans earlier that morning, but before he could answer, Julia spoke rapidly, as she always did.

"Yes, I'll do that. Come to think of it, Tania just wanted to meet Mike. I'll call and tell her it's off. Yes, it's settled. Just you and me. Dress casual; we are changing venue. Pick me up before eight. See you then."

With that, Julia hung up.

Frowning, Rudy looked at his dining table, where his review book sat opened. Julia really didn't give him much choice.

"No studying today. I guess I'm having dinner with Julia, alone," he said aloud to himself.

Rudy walked to the bathroom, thinking he would leave early and stop by Mike's place and pick up a change of clothes for tomorrow morning. Recalling quite well how his last meeting with Mike's dad had gone, Rudy decided he'd rather not have him answer the front door, not that he ever did. Rudy picked up the phone and called Mike's house. One thing was certain with the Davenports; they never answered their own phone. As expected, the house butler answered the call a few rings in.

"Davenport residence," the formal voice said in an impeccable fashion.

"Alfred, is that you?" Rudy asked.

"Mister Dell, what a pleasure to hear from you. How may I help you?" Alfred replied.

"Rudy, call me Rudy," Rudy insisted.

"Certainly, sir. How may I assist you?"

"Mike had to stay overnight at the hospital. Could you prepare a change of clothes for him?"

"Is he ill, or is this related to his studies?"

"He's on call."

"Very well. Should I have someone deliver them to the hospital?"

"No, I'll pick them up. I have to drive by anyway. Is a few minutes after seven okay?"

"Yes. Drive to the back entrance. I'll take them to your car personally. Would you care for something to eat? I could have something prepared."

"Not tonight. I'm going out to dinner later."

"Very well, sir. I look forward to seeing you."

Rudy was thankful that Alfred had offered to deliver Mike's clothes through the back entrance. Rudy's meetings with Mike's father had always been disturbing at best. The man was cold, calculating, and more concerned about the acquisition of money than anything else. Mike never spoke about his relationship with him, but Rudy could tell it was not a good one. On the other hand, Alfred, whom Rudy had learned had been with Mike's family since before Mike was born, was the exact opposite. From how often and the way Mike spoke about him, it was plain that Alfred was more of a father figure to Mike than his own father ever was.

***

It was a little after eight when Julia came down from her apartment. Rudy opened the Jeep's door for her, suddenly realizing he had left Mike's leather bag on the passenger seat. Rudy excused himself and reached for it, quickly placing it in the back seat. Julia then climbed in, turning to look at the bag behind her.

"That's for Mike. He was stuck at the hospital unexpectedly. I called Alfred and picked up a change of clothes," Rudy explained as he drove.

"Alfred," Julia said in an odd tone.

"What? He's cool," Rudy said.

"Mike's a billionaire. He has a butler who's almost like his father. The butler is named Alfred. Think about it; Mike could turn out to be Batman," Julia said, turning serious as she jumped into a dissertation to validate her theory.

They had just come up to a red light when Julia finished explaining her theory about Mike. Rudy couldn't help but laugh. Julia laughed loudly as well. As she did, her deep blue eyes caught Rudy's gaze and he noticed something he hadn't before. She had the slightest hint of a gummy smile. It didn't detract from her looks. On the contrary, it made her more so, and more human.

CHAPTER 4

Rudy wanted to make a good impression, so he set his alarm clock to sound off quite early. Unfortunately, he didn't get up when the alarm first sounded, sleeping for more than half an hour more. When Rudy finally managed to wake up, he realized he had overslept. He hurriedly jumped into action and left his apartment in such haste that he didn't have any breakfast.

As Rudy ran down to the oncology ward, he began to wonder if foregoing breakfast had been a mistake, as he was becoming quite hungry.

Yesterday, his encounter with Betances was such that he hadn't made it past the doors to the ward. Today he walked past the doors and up to the nurses' station. He checked his wristwatch and breathed a sigh of relief. It was a quarter to six. Not as early as he would have liked, but early enough. Behind the long counter sat a nurse, hunched over. She methodically wrote on a chart and ignored him. Excusing himself, Rudy asked for Mike.

"Keep walking, you'll find him," said the young nurse, who didn't bother to lift her gaze from her work.

Without another word, Rudy walked past the station and into the ward. As he expected, the walls were colorful, with bright drawings and pictures everywhere. Several small open areas lined the sides of the long hallway. In these areas most hospitals had chairs and couches for patients' family members to gather. Here they had been turned into play areas. Some of these had TVs, many already on, with cartoons glowing on their screens, but the volume turned all the way down.

It was so early that the halls were empty. Rudy scanned the lonely surroundings as he moved further inside the ward. Then, when he turned the first corner, Rudy came across a young mother helping a small boy as he walked. The boy, who couldn't have been more than seven, was bald and wore an oversized Yankees baseball shirt. His left hand held tightly to a metal IV pole on wheels. Attached at the top were several bags of clear fluid. Dangling from these, a few transparent IV lines met and merged into one. This last transparent plastic tube snaked down to his right arm, where it pierced his skin. The boy came to a stop just a few steps from Rudy. The boy stared at Rudy for a second. He seemed to be taking stock of him. Suddenly, the boy smiled.

"Hello," the boy said.

"Hi," replied Rudy.

"Who are you?" the boy asked.

"Ah, Rudy," Rudy replied absently.

"Just Rudy? Not a doctor or a nurse?" the boy asked, cocking his head.

"Well, no. I mean I'm a medical student," replied Rudy.

"What year?" the boy asked.

"Fourth," replied Rudy, wondering what the curious boy would say or ask next.

"Fourth year. Well, you're almost a doctor. Nice to meet you Doc Rudy, I'm Tim," replied the boy cheerfully.

"Nice to meet you too," Rudy replied as he smiled, utterly dumbfounded by the little boy.

"This is my mom, Olivia," Tim added.

"Pleasure," Rudy replied.

Olivia nodded, forcing a smile.

"Mom, can I watch TV now?" Tim asked.

Olivia nodded as she reached for the IV pole, but Tim pulled it towards him.

"I can do it," Tim said confidently.

"I know you can," Olivia replied.

Rudy then watched as the boy slowly limped to a chair near the silent TV. It was then that Rudy noticed his left leg was missing from the knee down, a red prosthetic covered in stickers in its place. Without thinking, he turned and met Olivia's gaze. With a weary and difficult smile, she spoke in a low voice.

"He's dealing really well with the leg. He wants to be the first pitcher with a prosthetic limb," Olivia said.

"With the Yankees?" Rudy asked.

Olivia nodded. Her eyes reddened, her smile unable to conceal her profound sadness.

"He seems to have the spirit for it," Rudy said.

Olivia grimaced, forcing a smile while she nodded slowly. She tried speaking, but it was clear she could not get the words out. For a long moment, she struggled before she managed to speak.

"Thank you," she said as she walked to join her son.

Rudy watched as the woman, who somehow looked older than she clearly was, sat next to the boy and placed her arm around him. Silently looking at the two, Rudy realized he wasn't feeling hungry anymore.

Moments later, Rudy came to the end of the ward and the doors to the small isolation ward. There, next to the door, was a small nurses' station. Sitting behind it was Mike. He had a few closed patient charts in front of him and wrote on the lone open chart on the counter in front of him. He wore bright green scrubs and looked tired. Rudy came closer, but Mike didn't seem to notice him.

"Hey," Rudy said.

Mike slowly raised his gaze. He wore a weary expression. His shoulders were sunken and Rudy noticed Mike looked tired— no, more than that, he looked drained. For a split second, Rudy was at a loss; then he remembered Tim. Rudy turned and looked down the long corridor and at all those doors. Behind every single one was a sick child, so it didn't take long for it to register. Rudy believed he now understood why Mike looked drained.

Rudy had come in ready to do rounds. He was eager to learn every patient's name, every condition. He wanted to be ready. After yesterday, Rudy had to impress Betances. But now, after meeting Tim and seeing Mike's solemn expression, trepidation won over eagerness. Rudy hesitated for a moment, and the fact that Mike didn't say anything made it all the more ominous. Placing Mike's small duffle bag on the counter, Rudy finally broke the silence.

"Here, Alfred packed a bag for you."

"Thanks."

"Don't mention it," Rudy replied as he placed his own bag behind the counter.

"Did you run into my father?" Mike said.

"Nope, I met Alfred at the kitchen's back entrance," Rudy replied, glad that he didn't, as it was something he had no desire to repeat.

"Looks like I lost the bet," someone said.

Rudy turned to see a snickering young nurse, who then walked away.

"What bet?" Rudy asked.

"That you wouldn't be here before rounds. I said that you would, so she lost," Mike said as he examined the contents of the duffle bag.

"What exactly did you win?" Rudy asked.

"I'm not sure," Mike said.

"Okay," Rudy replied.

"Did you call Julia?" Mike asked.

"Yeah, we went to dinner," Rudy replied.

"Good. I think she likes you," Mike said, smiling.

"Right," Rudy chuckled at the absurdity of the comment. He knew Mike was just trying to lighten the mood, so he let the comment slide. Although still apprehensive of what he would see today, Rudy knew that they had to get to work.

"Let's do some rounds. I want to be prepared before Betances gets here," Rudy said.

"He's already here. Well, not here, but in the hospital," Mike replied.

"Shit, why didn't you call me?" Rudy said.

"One of the patients took a turn for the worse last night. Betances came back a few minutes after midnight. We worked all night. The kid managed to pull through, but he's in surgery getting a tracheostomy. I don't think Betances will make it down here for quite some time," Mike replied.

Rudy was at a loss for words.

"Come on," Mike said, nodding. He got up, closed the plastic binder that held the patient chart inside, reached for the other charts, and moved in front of the counter. There Mike returned the charts to a small cart, which held the rest of the patient charts. There were eight in all. Above and below the patient charts were several small compartments filled with supplies of every kind. Mike then pulled the cart down the long hall, guiding it to the first room. Rudy followed closed behind. When they came to the first door, a nurse walked up and joined them.

"You Dell?" she asked.

Rudy nodded.

"Hathaway," she replied.

"Pleasure to meet you," Rudy replied.

Hathaway eyed Rudy as if trying to size him up before she spoke.

"We are not waking up these kids!" Hathaway said, and her tone was clear. She was stating fact.

"No. I just want to get a heads-up on the patients, see if there are any pending test results. If we need to get anything done today, we can get the ball rolling," Rudy replied, apparently not very convincingly.

"Is that so? I better go with you. Please take your bags to the lounge," Hathaway said with a mild degree of annoyance. She then turned to the other nurses at the station. "Ramirez, please join us, and bring all up-to-date labs."

"I printed everything just now," added Mike.

"Ramirez, do check for anything that's just arrived and join us," Hathaway said, not hiding her contempt.

Mike pushed the cart back to the main nurses' station. Rudy followed close behind, carrying both Mike's bag and his own. They came to a stop in front of the long counter. Rudy ran behind the counter and to the right down to a small hidden corridor that ran parallel to the main corridor. It did so only for fifteen feet, as it was all that was needed. It had a small lounge-meeting room, followed by a medication and supply room, and lastly the door to the small on-call room. Rudy placed the two bags in the lounge before running back to meet Mike.

Mike reached for the first chart and did a thorough case presentation on the young patient resting in the room behind them. Rudy wrote everything down in a small pocket notebook, making sure not to miss anything. Mike was about to elaborate on the treatment plan when the two other nurses finally joined them. Ramirez was in her early twenties and smiled pleasantly. Johansson, who Rudy recognized as the nurse who lost the bet to Mike, was a bit older, but not much, and wore a permanent frown. Hathaway exchanged looks with each of them, and then looked back at Mike.

"Well, Davenport. You seem to be right. Your results are all up-to-date," Hathaway said stoically.

Mike nodded silently and continued.

"He has been doing very well. We are waiting on today's labs. If they are okay, he'll be transferred down to the regular pediatric floor and home in a couple of days," Mike said.

"What labs?" Rudy asked, wanting to make a note.

"Don't worry, it's already done. They should be here before noon," Mike said reassuringly.

Rudy reached for the chart and searched until he found the lab orders, quickly making a note in his notebook.

"Just being thorough," Rudy said.

"Bull, you just want to have every answer," Mike said.

"Language, gentlemen," scolded Hathaway.

The group continued down the hall as Mike gave unabridged versions of every patient's history, current status, and treatment plan. Rudy quickly wrote down everything about their conditions—every single detail and lab result. Rudy did as he felt he needed to if he wanted to perform well in the clerkship. While they moved down the hall, Rudy silently organized his day. Since he needed to read up on every patient's condition, treatment, and prognosis, he tried to create a mental schedule of sorts. If he had been forced into this clerkship, he was going to make sure he shined. That was all that mattered.

Something unexpected happened as they moved down the hall. Rudy continued to write down every detail, but he felt his hand becoming heavier. Slower to write. Rudy also had some trouble getting the information down. Regardless of how hard he tried, his mind was unable to focus. His chest felt tight and his hand twitched at times.

Then they came to Tim's room, the little boy Rudy had met earlier that morning. As Mike began to review Tim's case, Rudy tried to speak, but he found it difficult, and although he could breathe, he found it was becoming labored.

"I met Tim just as I came in," Rudy said, surprised to hear his voice breaking slightly.

Mike nodded knowingly before he continued.

"Rhabdomyosarcoma, left leg. He had an amputation and chemo eighteen months ago. A week ago his surgeon found a mass above his knee. He was started on the experimental chemotherapy protocol Doctor Betances is working on. An excisional biopsy was performed two days ago. We are waiting on the pathology. They are doing several tests, DNA, all sorts of things. Betances wants at least three pathologists to confirm independently. He wants to be sure," Mike said.

Rudy looked down at his notebook, but only managed to stare at the blank page for a moment. He did write *rhabdomyo-sarcoma* but was unable to write the details. With some difficulty he managed to write Tim's name, but nothing else. Not that he saw a need to. Rudy was sure he would never forget anything about Tim, even if he tried. It dawned on him that there was the distinct possibility that he might have to deal with losing a patient in the next few weeks, a child. Suddenly his enthusiasm, or rather his hurry to get on with rounds, started to dwindle.

"Are you guys done talking about me?" Tim said, surprising everyone.

"Good morning, Tim." Mike pointed to Rudy. "You met Rudy, right?"

"Yup," Tim said as he walked into his room, followed closely by his mother Olivia, who smiled politely at the group. Then, as if an idea just occurred to him, Tim turned.

"Rudy, are you a Yankees fan?" Tim asked, his face now serious.

"You'll have to excuse Rudy. He's not a sports fan, more of a nerd," said Mike.

The strange remark caught Rudy by surprise.

"That's okay, as long as he's not a Red Sox fan," Tim said.

Rudy chuckled; he was so very surprised by Tim's comments. Despite the gravity of his situation, Tim seemed to be more preoccupied by the Yankees and the Red Sox. Despite it all, despite his illness, Tim went on with his life. The things that were important to him still mattered.

"I'm not," Rudy said.

"Cool," Tim said, clearly delighted.

"Do you mind if we check your leg?" Mike asked.

"Okay," Tim said, shrugging.

The group followed Tim inside, but waited for him to climb into bed. His mother stood at his side but allowed him to climb into bed by himself, which he did with surprising agility and ease.

Mike removed the prosthetic limb and carefully examined the biopsy wound, clearly checking for infection and inflammation. Rudy observed closely.

"Everything looks fine," Mike said.

Olivia helped Tim get his prosthetic limb back on. Tim then reached for a small electronic device. It beeped when he turned it on.

"You know the rules," Olivia said.

"Mom, I'm not hungry," Tim complained as he placed the device back on the bed beside him.

"What's that?" Rudy asked, looking at the cream-colored device.

Smiling, Tim reached for the device and turned it on.

"It's a Game Boy!" Tim said excitedly.

"What's a Game Boy?" Rudy asked.

"Here!" Tim handed Rudy the device. "It's a Nintendo. You play with these controls. I have more games."

Looking intently at the small screen, Rudy read the name of the game. "Tetris?" he asked.

"It's really cool. Go ahead play it," Tim said.

"I can't right now, but I'll take you up on that. I'll come by later," Rudy said.

"Before you go?" Tim asked.

"I'm on call, so I'll be here all night," Rudy replied.

"Oh!" Tim said excitedly. "We'll be watching *The Sandlot* later. You can come watch it with us."

"If I get some time I'll swing by. You can teach me about that game," Rudy replied.

Tim smiled and gave Rudy a cheerful thumbs-up, then he frowned.

"Are you going to see Maria?" Tim asked.

"Just now," Mike replied.

"Will you say hi for me?" Tim said with a sad look.

"Will do, buddy," Mike said before they left the room.

Once outside, Mike placed Tim's chart back on the cart. While Mike explained Tim's options, Rudy found himself involuntarily reaching for his chest. It was then that he realized Mike's voice seemed somehow distant, but just for a moment. Then it suddenly boomed.

"Rudy, you okay?" Mike asked.

"Yeah, I just suddenly felt out of breath," Rudy said.

"Yeah, happened to me last night. As I was saying, we need to wait for the biopsy results," Mike replied.

"Who's Maria? One of the nurses?" Rudy asked.

"No, she's our next patient," Mike said as he pointed to the doors leading to the isolation ward.

CHAPTER 5

Mike was about to start going over Maria's case when Betances joined them.

After hearing that he had spent most of the night in the hospital, Rudy half expected to see Betances drained, but the opposite was true. He looked as if nothing had happened. His clothes told another story. Betances still wore his white coat, but unlike yesterday, he wore rumpled scrubs under it. He walked silently, carrying a large coffee mug, which he didn't drink from.

"Dell," Betances said, acknowledging him without a single glance.

"How's the boy doing?" asked Hathaway.

"Not well. He was moved to ICU, full ventilator. Organ failure has set in," Betances said in a monotone.

Hathaway closed her eyes for a second as if saying a silent prayer before she spoke again.

"Do the parents know?" Hathaway asked.

Betances nodded. "They do, but they need time."

"There isn't much," Hathaway replied.

Betances nodded knowingly as he placed his coffee on the counter. For a long uncomfortable moment, everyone was silent.

It was then that Rudy thought about his so-called medical career. Up to this moment, everything had been a challenge. He had learned to see patients as tests of his abilities. Rudy saw them not as people, but as problems to be solved, unconsciously rationalizing away the human factor, the empathy. Only then could he be in control of the situation, only then could he help them, or so he thought. People got sick, they had accidents, and he as a doctor would do his best to help them. Believing this, Rudy had learned to be caring but unattached.

"If you become attached, you may compromise. You will lose focus, and that's how people die. Nothing can cloud your judgment; you can't allow it," a surgeon had told him about a year ago.

Rudy had taken this to heart and had been all the better for it. This he truly believed. Up until now, he had never truly faced death. He had seen his fair share, but they had been patients with whom he had little interaction, people he had never really met, nor gotten to know. His fourth-year surgical rotation had been spent dealing with trauma, and his internal medicine rotation was scheduled for March, almost at the end of the year. So he had yet to experience the loss of a longstanding patient, not yet at least, and certainly not a child.

"Tim?" asked Betances, breaking the silence.

"All the lab work is excellent; very few side effects from the chemo," replied Mike.

Betances eyed Mike for a moment, turning to Nurse Hathaway a second later. She nodded as if answering a question only she had heard. Rudy noticed the exchange. It was plain; Betances did not trust Mike.

"Pathology?" asked Hathaway.

"Nothing yet," replied Betances.

"Let's say hi to Maria," Betances said as he moved past the doors and into the isolation area.

The double doors separated isolation from the main hallway. Past them there was a small hallway, a door to each side and one at the very end, three rooms in total. Beside each door there was a cart full of supplies and a crash cart.

Betances walked up to a cart and reached for a disposable facemask, hairnet, and shoe covers. He quickly and expertly donned them. On cue, everyone followed suit, with Mike and Rudy taking the longest. Without waiting, Betances pushed the first door on the left and walked inside. The nurses followed closely, then Mike. Rudy walked inside last.

As Rudy came into the room he was surprised. He expected to find the isolation room cold and spartan, but it was far from it. The walls were brightly colored, with drawings taped on them. On the wall beside the door to the bathroom there were several instant photographs arranged and taped together. All showed smiling children, all bald. The room had a window with the usual blinds found in any hospital, but pink curtains adorned the window frames. In one corner was a small television with a VCR on top and some tapes below it. A few toys rested on a shelf above the TV. A bed with a sliding desk and a reclining chair beside it made up most of the room's furniture.

The small bed was right in the middle of the room. Behind the bed, a metal column bolted to the floor extended up to the ceiling. On it hung various monitors and hooks for saline bags and medication.

The small sliding desk was about halfway up from the foot of the bed. On top of it, a couple of books, coloring pencils, and blank paper rested beside a framed photo of a couple of kids on a farm. Hunched over the desk was a little girl, drawing. She continued drawing, ignoring her visitors for a moment, but then slowly and deliberately she raised her head. Rudy noticed she wore the most sincere smile he had ever seen.

The smiling girl behind the table wore faded pink pajamas, which suited her. Her head was completely bald and slightly tilted to the right. She wore a pink headband decorated with several embroidered flowers. She was clearly weak, thin, and pale, but her smile beamed. In contrast to her complexion, her large eyes hadn't lost their sparkle, glowing as she smiled.

"Hello, Doctor Betances. How are you?" she asked, pronouncing the doctor's last name perfectly.

"Very well, Maria, and you?" Betances replied.

"Good," Maria replied, pointing at Rudy. "Is he a doctor or medical student?"

"Dell is a fourth-year medical student, just like Davenport. He'll be helping us take care of you," Betances replied.

Maria crossed her thin arms and spoke.

"Come on, Doc. Another one?" Maria replied. She forced a frown as she tried to hide her smile.

"But you are my best attending," Betances replied.

"I think we need to examine our business arrangement. The deal was for one student, not two," Maria continued, clearly having trouble hiding her smile.

Rudy repeated the phrase in his mind—*examine our business arrangement*. He couldn't believe the little girl had just said that.

"I'll see what I can do. The economy is bad right now. What could I do to persuade you?" Betances said, feigning contemplation.

"A box of crayons, a big one!" Maria said.

"Twenty-four crayons?" Betances gave a low whistle. "That might be difficult."

"No, no, the big one, sixty-four crayons," Maria replied.

"Sixty-four, I don't know if I can manage that," Betances said, shaking his head.

"You can teach them all by yourself," Maria said, forcing an unconvincing glare. Despite her obvious attempts to stop them, a few giggles escaped her.

"Okay, okay, you drive a hard bargain." With that, Betances reached into one of the lower pockets of his lab coat and produced the large box containing sixty-four crayons. Making a show of it, he placed it on the table.

An excited Maria reached for the top of the box and opened it. She examined every color. Carefully, she ran her small, thin fingers over the tips of the crayons. She then lovingly closed the box and brought it to her chest, closing her hands around it.

"Thank you," she said.

People said thank you all the time, mostly because of social conventions or compromise. However Rudy could see that what he had just witnessed was a true expression of gratitude. From what he could see, this gift meant the world to the girl.

"I'll bring some new coloring books tomorrow. How's that?" Betances asked.

"You don't have to," Maria replied.

"No, but I will. Anything else you need?" Betances asked.

"No," Maria replied, again touching the big box of crayons.

"Anything else you want? Maybe some blank notebooks to draw in?" Betances asked.

Maria's eyes beamed, but she shook her head.

"I still have some room in the old ones," she replied as she flipped the pages of one of her notebooks.

"Nonsense, you can never have enough notebooks. I'll bring some," Betances said, smiling.

"Thank you," Maria said.

"You bet." Betances's voice turned serious. "'Examine our business arrangement.' Where did you get that?" he added, forcing a fake scowl.

Maria busted out in a mixture of giggles and laughter.

"*Sixty Minutes*," she said, shrugging.

"Keeping current with world events?" Betances said, shaking his head.

A smiling Maria nodded enthusiastically.

"Good, that's important. Mind if I examine you so we can get out of your hair?" Betances said.

Maria nodded again, but her smile faded.

As Betances examined the little girl, Rudy noticed that he did so with great care, even lovingly. He also noticed that Betances did not say anything while he examined Maria. This was different than his past experiences, when attendings would point out findings as they came up during physical examinations.

When he finished, Betances smiled before he spoke. "Excellent. We are now going outside to gossip about you. I'll be back in a while."

"Promise?" Maria asked, her eyes sparkling as she smiled.

"Try and stop me. Please eat," Betances said, pointing to a tray held by Nurse Johansson.

Maria frowned as she looked at the food on the tray, but nodded slowly. She then carefully gathered her drawings and set them beside her on the bed. Once the desk had some free space, Johansson placed the tray on the sliding desk.

"Some TV, honey?" Hathaway asked.

Maria nodded.

"No *Sixty Minutes*," Betances said loudly.

Maria giggled, then turned to Rudy. "Nice to meet you."

"You too," Rudy replied.

Before he left the room, Rudy gazed back. He thought he was the last one inside, but he noticed that Johansson stayed behind. The nurse walked to the television and flipped through the channels until Maria signaled her to stop. Johansson then sat next to the bed and started to talk to Maria.

CHAPTER 6

When Rudy finally walked outside the room, he found Betances reaching for his coffee. He raised the cup to his mouth but paused midway, eyeing Rudy as he moved closer. Betances raised his left hand and pointed at his head, then at Rudy's. Bemused, Rudy slowly reached for his head, feeling the paper hat he still wore. Surprised and embarrassed, Rudy quickly removed it, crushing it into a ball before throwing it inside a trash bin.

"Thanks," he said.

Betances nodded as he again raised the cup to his mouth. Rudy watched, thinking that the coffee must be cold and tasteless by now. He expected Betances to taste it and throw it away, but he didn't. Betances just stared at the cup for a moment before he placed it back on the counter. He then turned his attention to Mike and Rudy.

"Maria is almost ten years old. She has end-stage leukemia. She responded to treatment initially, but as soon as the treatment was completed, it recurred. We tried everything. I won't bore you with the details. It's all in her chart. Her condition is unresponsive to treatment."

"Nothing?" Mike asked.

"Chemo, bone marrow transplants, even experimental drug trials . . . nothing. My main concern right now is keeping her happy and comfortable," Betances said.

"Family?" Mike asked.

"No." Betances removed his glasses. "Maria was abandoned in the same hospital where she was born. Her mother just showed up in full labor. She gave a fake name and disappeared soon after. So she's a ward of the state, and has spent most of her life in government-run orphanages. Maria did live with a few foster families for a while, but most of these families were not meant to be permanent; some only take the children in for the paycheck. She jumped around in the system for a few years and finally ended up on a farm up north. An elderly couple, the Millers, fostered her. She spent almost three years with them, and from what she tells me she was very happy there. It seems they didn't see her as a paycheck."

"The picture—she is the one in the picture—that's her on the farm?" Rudy said.

Betances nodded.

"What happened? Because she was sick they sent her back?" Rudy asked, immediately regretting his phrasing.

Betances glared at Rudy for a few seconds.

"No, Mr. Miller died. Apparently his wife had been suffering from Alzheimer's. He had been taking care of her and the children. Once he was gone, the children were far too much for her," Betances said.

"The children?" Mike asked.

"There was also a boy," Betances replied.

"The boy in the photo," Rudy noted.

Betances nodded.

"Billy. Her brother," Betances replied. "Not her actual brother, but just as well. A foster kid as well, just a few years older than her. He was already there when she arrived. Maria seemed to have bonded with him. The way she speaks about him, I think he was her whole world. They came back to the orphanage together. When she first got sick, one of the social workers would bring Billy to see her. One day he just stopped coming," Betances said as he reached for her chart.

"We sent our own social worker to find out what happened. It was then that we found out Billy had been adopted," Hathaway said in a low voice. "I was the one who told Maria. She's just a kid. I didn't know how she would take it." Hathaway shook her head. "Maria was so happy for him. No resentment. She was only sad because he wouldn't come around anymore."

"Did he move away?" Rudy asked.

"They wouldn't tell us," Hathaway replied in a broken voice.

"How long ago?" Mike asked.

"More than nine months. She doesn't really have anyone," Hathaway replied, her voice now strained.

"She's been here in the hospital for the better part of a year. Since she's a ward of the state, this place is her home, these people her family. What little she has in her room are gifts from the staff and from the parents of the other children," Betances said.

"Doc, you too," Hathaway said, nodding.

Betances shook his head as he waved her off before he continued. "The hospital's budget is stretched thin. We have TVs in the common areas, but most parents get their kids a small TV and some video games. She only has us and what we can give her," Betances said.

"I made her the pink curtains," Hathaway's voice caught for a moment. "The TV was a gift from Jenny's parents. Jenny said she wanted her friend Maria to have it," Hathaway grimaced, her expression hardening.

"She gave her the TV when she was discharged?" asked Mike.

Rudy noticed Hathaway staring at Mike blankly. Betances didn't stare; he just took a deep, silent breath. In an instant, Rudy felt a sharp stab of understanding.

"No, when she passed," Rudy said.

Betances nodded silently.

Rudy's chest tightened upon voicing his realization. There was an infinitesimal moment when a furious multitude of thoughts raced through Rudy's mind. It was clear to him that nothing he had done before had prepared him for this. Rudy had to admit that this might be more that he could bear. He had never questioned his medical career before. Now, for the first time since he started medical school, he questioned the path he had chosen. Before, he had convinced himself he could remain detached. Now he wondered if he ever could, or if he would want to. He cringed, enraged, but only internally. He swore to himself that he would face this challenge as he had all others. Still, he was sure that this would be his toughest test. Perhaps he might come to learn he was not meant to be a doctor.

"More than you expected?" Betances remarked as if reading Rudy's mind.

Rudy silently acknowledged him, turning to see Mike nodding as well.

"We'll see if you measure up," Betances said.

"Is there any way to find her brother?" Rudy asked.

Betances shook his head.

"He's a minor. All adoption records are sealed. We tried. Believe me, we tried," Hathaway said.

"Billy, William . . . How about a last name?" Rudy asked.

"Roberts, why?" Hathaway asked.

"I have a friend. He is a lawyer, a good one. Maybe he can help us," Rudy said.

"Billy might have a new last name, but if you think he can help . . ." Hathaway said.

Something in Hathaway's tone, which was less than encouraging, did not reassure Rudy. Maybe they had already tried this but couldn't get themselves to admit it was useless. He felt he needed to try.

"Dell, Davenport, follow me. Hathaway, make sure Maria eats something," Betances said as he moved down the corridor.

"Where are we going?" Rudy asked, instantly realizing he was crazy for asking.

Betances turned and glared at Mike and Rudy in frank annoyance. His expression then turned to amusement. "To work, Doctor Dell, to work."

With that, Betances turned and stormed off. Mike and Rudy followed close behind. Once outside the oncology ward, Betances addressed them.

"Have you ever done a bone marrow biopsy?" Betances asked without turning.

"No," Mike and Rudy replied.

"Today, you will," Betances said in a most foreboding tone.

CHAPTER 7

Taking care of hospital consults took most of the day. It was late afternoon when they finally headed back to the oncology ward. Rudy felt exhausted and dreaded the rest of his day, as he was on call. Without meaning to, he had skipped lunch. Despite not having breakfast, Rudy didn't feel very hungry. This might have been surprising a week ago, but not now, not here. Not after what he had seen today.

As the group moved back to the oncology ward, Betances's pager beeped loudly. He reached blindly into his right coat pocket, producing the buzzing device in a flash. His eyes scanned the small glowing screen as he read the message, he then silently dropped the pager back into his pocket. He then motioned everyone to follow him down the hospital hall. Led by him, Mike and Rudy followed, walking quickly abreast. They came to a nurses' station next to the pediatric ICU. Betances walked up to the counter, reached for the phone, and dialed a number from memory. He didn't greet anyone, nor did he speak, at least as far as Rudy could tell. Betances just stood there, listening intently. Then he spoke.

"I'm on my way."

Now walking faster, the group finally reached the oncology ward. Betances pushed open the double doors, walking down the hall and into one of the rooms. It was a room they had visited earlier in the day—Megan's.

Once inside, Rudy saw Megan drawing on the sliding desk over her bed. Her father Bruce, whom Rudy had met earlier in the day, sat next to her. Bruce forced a smile. He was red-faced, and his expression was a haphazard mix of emotions, but gloom won over.

As soon as Megan saw Betances, she smiled at him and proudly showed him her drawing.

"That's a great drawing. I love it," Betances said as he sat next to Megan, smiling imperceptibly at her father. Bruce acknowledged it with a small nod, which Rudy could have sworn was a silent thank-you.

"That's a bus, a Ferris wheel, and I bet I know what that is," Betances said, pointing at the drawing.

Megan giggled, bobbing her head in excitement.

"Yeah!" Betances said, grinning.

"Megan, I heard a rumor, something about you not wanting to have an IV. I told them I couldn't believe that, not from my star patient," Betances said with great empathy.

Megan took a deep breath and rubbed the inside of her arm before she spoke.

"It's . . . it's Nurse Paul. I tried to explain, but she didn't listen. I told her, but she wanted to do it her way, and I said no," Megan replied.

"Why?" Betances asked softly.

Megan slouched as she ran her finger up and down her arm. She then gave everyone a detailed description of most of the veins and arteries in her arm, which was then followed by her explanation of why she didn't let the nurse place the IV.

"I told her the vein she wanted to use is broken. I told her she had to use this one. This one is good," Megan said as she ran her finger over the side of her arm, sulking in frustration.

Betances nodded, pursing his lips.

"Of course, any fool knows that," he said, nodding. "I'll straighten this up." He got up and walked out of the room. Then, as the door was about to close behind him, Betances turned.

"Megan, why don't you explain your beautiful drawing to those two? They are rather slow," he added, pointing to Mike and Rudy before he left.

Rudy knew this was meant to keep Megan distracted while Betances dealt with the situation. He moved closer to Megan, but not before looking at Bruce. As if understanding, Megan's dad nodded, giving silent permission for Rudy and then Mike to move closer to the girl.

"Hey, Megan, tell me about your drawing," Mike said.

"See, that's the bus. It's driving us over to Disneyland. See, that's the Ferris wheel," Megan suddenly frowned, as if thinking for a moment. "Are there Ferris wheels at Disneyland?" she asked.

"No, but the rides are better than any Ferris wheels," Rudy replied, smiling.

"Really?" Megan asked, her sunken eyes sparkling.

"Yes. Lots of rides, all fun, even a few roller coasters," Rudy replied.

Megan frowned. "I'm too small for those."

"Not for all of them, and then there is a cruise through the jungle, and the pirates. That one is my favorite. Oh, and the haunted mansion too," Rudy said with true excitement.

Megan's eyes opened wide.

"Is it scary?" she asked.

"A little, but a lot of fun," Rudy said.

"I'm brave, I think," Megan said with determination.

Rudy smiled. Words failed him for the moment. From the little time he had been with these kids, he had learned one thing: they were the bravest people he had ever known. He had been wondering if he would be as brave when his time came, when he too would have to face his own mortality.

"Will I see Mickey?" Megan asked.

The question pulled Rudy back. He gazed at Mike, who stood across from him smiling at the little girl, and nodded silently.

"Yes, you will," Rudy replied.

Megan giggled as she returned to her drawing. Rudy noticed the bus in the drawing had people's faces drawn in it, so he pointed to the drawing and asked Megan about it.

"That's us riding on the bus," Megan replied.

"Us?" asked Rudy.

Megan bobbed her head and pointed to the faces.

"That's me, this is Tim, that's Dough, and that's Maria," Megan said as she turned to look at Rudy.

It was then that Rudy noticed something. He realized that all the passengers were bald, but before he could say anything or really process it, Betances walked back in with Nurse Ramirez.

"All settled. You won't mind if Ramirez gets that IV going," Betances said.

Nurse Ramirez walked in behind Betances. She smiled pleasantly as she greeted everyone. Megan sighed, but forced a smile in return. She pushed her sliding desk away and down the bed so she could turn and sit on the side of the bed. Ramirez moved closer. She carried a small red tray full of supplies with her.

After setting the tray down, Ramirez got to work setting up her work area. She gave Megan a set of gloves, which the girl put on. Ramirez then reached for a small alcohol swab and handed it to Megan. In a swift motion, Megan expertly cleaned the area around the side of her arm, the same area she had told Nurse Paul to use for the IV. While she did that, Nurse Ramirez set up a small saline bag on a long plastic IV tube and made sure the liquid moved down the tube and out the far side. She then handed Megan some sterile gauze, which she used to carefully dry any remaining alcohol on her arm. Rudy frowned as he watched Megan.

"It hurts more if it's still wet," remarked Megan as if reading his thoughts.

"Ready?" asked Ramirez.

Megan nodded, stretched her arm out, and closed her eyes tightly.

Ramirez went to work rapidly. Megan didn't make a sound, and in an instant Ramirez set up a working IV exactly where Megan had pointed out.

"Is that okay?" Ramirez asked.

Megan examined the IV and carefully flexed her arm, nodding with satisfaction afterwards. Ramirez reached into her little tray and produced a small cup with two white pills inside.

"Take those. I'll be by in a while," Ramirez said before she left.

"Is that so I don't get sick?" Megan asked.

Betances nodded. Megan shook her head slowly but didn't say anything. Betances drew a deep breath and moved closer to Megan, speaking almost in a whisper.

"I know, but you can have anything you want for dinner, even ten pounds of ice cream," Betances then made a show of glaring at Bruce. "I don't care what that guy says."

Megan's eyes widened, and she quickly turned to her father, who smiled in approval. A smiling Megan then turned back to Betances, who gave her a thumbs-up.

"I'll see you later, Megan. If you have time, draw me a beach. I love the beach," Betances said.

Megan returned the thumbs-up. She then turned away from the side of the bed, pulling her sliding desk towards her. Reaching for a blank paper, Megan dove into it with intent as she began to draw. Betances smirked in satisfaction and motioned Mike and Rudy to follow him. Rudy followed Mike, who was in turn behind Betances. As they walked out of the room, Rudy turned and addressed Megan and Bruce.

"I'll be back later too. I'm on call, so anything you guys need just let me know," Rudy said.

"Thank you," Bruce replied.

Without raising her gaze, Megan gave Rudy a thumbs-up and continued drawing.

Rudy came out last, only to find Betances in a confrontation with a tall nurse whom he had not seen before.

"This is the last time you send one of your students to practice IV access in this ward, are we clear?" Betances said forcefully.

"Ray, be reasonable. These kids need to have access changed frequently. Where better for my nursing students to get much-needed experience and you get the help?" the tall nurse said.

"These kids are going through hell. I will not allow you to inflict any more pain than is absolutely necessary. No more students. Understood?" Betances said forcefully.

"We'll see about that," the tall nurse said, storming out.

"I'm sorry, Doc. I tried to stop them," Hathaway said apologetically.

Betances slowly nodded. "I'll take care of this. If she or any students show up again, call me," he added sternly.

"I will," Hathaway said.

Rudy was suddenly startled when Betances turned in his direction.

"Dell, Davenport, let's check on everyone before I leave," Betances said as he rushed down the hall.

Mike and Rudy were following close behind Betances when they heard a voice.

"Doctor Dell," the voice called.

Everyone turned to see Bruce standing a few feet outside his door.

"Is everything okay?" asked Rudy.

Bruce moved closer, forcing a smile.

"I just wanted to thank you. For what you told Megan about Disneyland. She is even more excited now," Bruce said, his discouraged expression surfacing despite his clear efforts to hide it. "It's so good to see her happy," he added before he suddenly reached for Rudy and hugged him tightly.

"Thank you, thank you," he said as he held on to Rudy. Taken by surprise, Rudy could do nothing but return the gesture as he felt his heart sink and a deep weight fall on his chest. Bruce released him. "I'm sorry, Doc, it's just—"

"It's okay," Rudy said, now fighting the urge to break down, before continuing. "I'm glad I could do something."

Bruce nodded, again forcing an unconvincing smile, and silently walked back inside their room, back to Megan.

A heavy silence fell on all those present. After a moment, it was broken by Betances.

"You okay?" Betances asked.

"I'm fine," Rudy said absently. But he wasn't; he wasn't fine at all.

"Hathaway," called Betances.

"Already ahead of you," Hathaway said as she came out from the little pantry beside the nurses' station. She carried a large coffee mug in her hand. She pushed the large mug into Rudy's hand. He stared at it as hot steam rose all around his face. It smelled appetizing, but Rudy didn't feel like drinking it.

"No, I'm okay, really, but thank you anyway," Rudy replied absently.

"Take it and drink it," Betances ordered. "We didn't have any lunch, and I'm sure you won't have any dinner."

After a deep sigh, Rudy took a sip of the coffee, cringing as the intense flavor hit him. It was painfully sweet.

"It's actually more sugar than coffee, but you need the energy. Drink up," Hathaway said.

Rudy understood. No lunch, and after what had just happened, whatever appetite he might have had vanished. So with some reluctance, he drank the coffee.

"Good, can't have you falling down tonight. Let's get on with it," Betances said.

Rudy walked behind him, still dazed, when he heard Mike's voice.

"Doctor Betances, that trip she's going on, it's her"—Mike hesitated—"last wish?"

"Those children are not responding to treatment as we hoped. The foundation decided to push the trip forward while they are still strong enough," Betances said without turning. He didn't stop walking either.

"Do the parents understand?" Mike asked.

"The children are very aware of what this means, more so than their parents," Betances replied.

CHAPTER 8

The better part of an hour had elapsed before they set out to begin the afternoon rounds. Mike was helping Rudy gather the charts when a doctor Rudy had not seen before joined them. After shaking hands with Betances, the new doctor addressed Mike and Rudy.

"Who's Davenport?" he asked.

Rudy nodded slightly toward Mike.

"And you are?" he asked, turning to Rudy.

"Dell."

"I'm Doctor Andropov."

He was a pediatric oncology fellow. He had been out with the flu. As such, he could not work among the immunosuppressed patients, and could not return until he was no longer contagious. He had been fine for the last four days, but the head of infectious disease wanted him to wait. Having just been cleared by them, he rushed to the ward, eager to return to work.

"Go home. It's late. Start tomorrow," Betances said.

Andropov smiled, turned away, and walked down the hall in the direction of the rooms. After a few steps, he turned and motioned everyone to follow him. It was clear he had no intention of going home.

Rudy was surprised by how fast they finished the afternoon rounds. Things ran smoothly, which was in no small part the result of Betances's methodical and organized approach. Nevertheless, Betances made a point of spending all the time needed with every patient. It was not unusual for him to deal with far more than just their medical ailments.

Once the afternoon rounds were over, Betances, Andropov, Mike, and Rudy moved into the small pantry behind the main nurses' counter. Once there, they all sat at a small table.

Rudy produced the list of things to do during the night call, which was exceedingly small. Betances had a rule: unless it was a matter of life or death, all treatment and procedures were to be done early in the morning. This gave ample time to deal with any occurrence or anything that happened while everyone was there and all the hospital services were running at full speed.

The group went down the list one by one and discussed their plans for the following day. Once the meeting was over, Andropov offered to stay on call.

"That's okay, I already have all my stuff here," Rudy replied, which was true, but there was another reason. As it was Friday, Rudy could leave after morning rounds the next day. Furthermore, he wouldn't have to come in on Sunday as rounds would be handled by those on call.

"Fine. Dell, just check on everyone at least once during the night. The nurses here are excellent. They won't call on you unless it is completely necessary," Andropov said.

"It's true. They were very helpful last night," Mike added.

Betances, who had excused himself from the table a few minutes before, came back, followed by a nurse Rudy hadn't seen before.

"Dell, this is Chen. She will be in charge of the next shift," Betances said.

"Pleasure," Rudy replied, looking at Chen.

Chen smiled but didn't say anything, leaving soon after.

"Chen's doing a shift at the blood bank. She'll be here in a few hours for the next shift. At four a.m., she will help you set up a blood transfusion. She will then help you watch for any reactions. If anything happens, call for the resident running the ICU. The crash cart will be at the bedside and has everything you need," Betances said.

"Who is getting the transfusion?" Rudy asked.

"Maria," Betances said.

The room fell into a silent contemplation.

"Wouldn't it be better to wait until we are all here?" asked Andropov. "We can come in early."

"If this works, that's the time she will be transfused again," Betances said.

"Again?" Rudy asked.

"If we manage to get her counts up with the transfusion and they hold, maybe she can make a trip to Disneyland. This is her last chance," Betances said.

Everyone nodded silently.

***

It was a few hours later when Rudy finished his to-do list. He then sat in the main nurses' station going over the patients' charts. After writing the evening notes, he made sure to write orders for the early morning labs. Rudy then checked Maria's chart, going over the orders for her upcoming transfusion. He was almost done when he noticed Nurse Hathaway walking up to him.

"I thought you were off," Rudy said, surprised.

"I am. I stayed a while with Maria," Hathaway replied.

For a second, Rudy wondered why, but rapidly understood.

"Here!" Hathaway said, handing Rudy a paper bag and a coffee.

Rudy accepted it and peered inside the bag, where he found a large muffin.

"There's other stuff in the lounge down the hall. I'm guessing you are going to forget about dinner tonight," Hathaway said.

She was right. Despite not having real food since yesterday, Rudy still didn't feel very hungry.

"Thank you. That's very kind of you," Rudy replied.

"Try to get some sleep. It's usually quiet here, but you never know," Hathaway said.

Rudy had done horribly long night calls before. He had spent countless hours in emergency rooms, operating rooms, and ICUs, during which he had been faced with never-ending work and terrible situations. But at no time had he ever felt so much uneasiness as he felt now. The thought of being here terrified him. As before, he wasn't sure how he would react if anything went wrong. Before it had been a challenge, but he no longer saw it that way. If he was sure of one thing, it was that he now felt fear, and he had never felt it before.

Suddenly, a pager in Hathaway's purse went off. She reached for it, read the message, and smiled.

"My husband just got out of surgery. I'll see you tomorrow," Hathaway said.

"Is he okay?" Rudy replied.

Hathaway smiled reassuringly. "He is a surgeon. Our kids are away at college, so I usually wait for him to finish." Hathaway turned and looked down the hall. "If I can, I help around here. Lately I have been spending time with Maria." Hathaway again turned and looked down the hall. It was very clear to Rudy that she was looking at the doors to isolation. Forcing a smile, she turned back to Rudy.

"Can I ask for a favor?"

"Sure," Rudy replied as he took a sip of the over-sugared coffee. The warm liquid tasted invigorating, making Rudy realize he was famished. Still, he didn't feel like eating.

"If you have some free time, go sit with Maria. You could take a few charts and work on them with her. I do. It's just she's there all by herself," Hathaway said.

Rudy wanted to use the down time to get some studying done, which he desperately needed to do. For a second he hesitated. Then, without thinking, he replied, "I will," surprising himself, as he wasn't planning to say that. Regardless, he had, and if this veteran nurse wanted him to do this, he would. He could spare a little time.

"Thank you," Hathaway said.

It struck Rudy that her eyes conveyed an emotion he seldom saw when people asked for favors; he saw true gratitude. He didn't know how to respond, so he just smiled. Her pager went off again.

"See you tomorrow," Hathaway said and slowly left.

Rudy was still unsure as to why he had agreed, but he had, and he was true to his word. He downed the rest of the coffee while he finished some notes. The muffin didn't appeal to him, so he decided to save it for later. After placing the charts back on the cart, Rudy went into the little on call room where he had left his things. Rummaging inside his small bag, Rudy looked for his USMLE review book. It wasn't difficult to find, as he had very few things inside. Book in hand, Rudy headed to check on the patients.

Rudy visited every patient's room, including Tim's, who gave him a small review of the New York Yankees' history while he was there. Rudy had no clue as to the team's history, but guessed that Tim's account was more than accurate. He also visited Megan and Bruce, who were now joined by Megan's mother. Megan triumphantly showed Rudy the drawing she had made for Doctor Betances.

"That's perfect," Rudy said.

"Seriously?" Megan asked.

"Yeah, it's really great," Rudy said.

"I can draw something for you," Megan said.

Rudy wasn't used to these interactions. Adults sometimes offered things out of courtesy, expecting people to decline. But with children, Rudy wasn't sure. However, Megan's expression made him quite certain she wanted him to say yes.

"I would love that, but only if it's no trouble," Rudy replied.

Megan giggled. "What do you want me to draw?"

"A Jeep?" Rudy asked.

Megan nodded playfully.

"Thank you," Rudy said, turning to the parents. "If you need anything, just let me know."

Rudy then left the small family and headed to isolation, where he would visit his last patient, and where he planned to stay for a while.

Past the isolation doors, Rudy donned the protective gear. Despite knowing these were meant to protect Maria, he wondered if they didn't make the poor girl feel further isolated.

Once he was ready, Rudy knocked softly on the door, not wanting to wake Maria if it happened that she was sleeping.

"Yes!" the quick reply came back.

Rudy pushed the door open and found Maria wide awake, smiling at him.

CHAPTER 9

"May I come in?" asked Rudy, smiling back.

"Yes."

Rudy walked in and was surprised when he noticed Nurse Bellaire sitting on the reclining chair next to Maria. Rudy had met Bellaire when her shift started, about an hour ago. She, along with the rest of her crew, would be taking care of the ward for the next eight hours. While she sat beside Maria, clipboard on her lap, she seemed to be taking care of some paperwork. As soon as Rudy walked in, she interrupted her work. Unsure of how to proceed, Rudy allowed himself to say the first thing that popped into his mind.

"Do you mind if I keep Maria company for a while?" Rudy asked.

Bellaire eyed Rudy for a moment, then after quickly organizing her paperwork on the clipboard, she got up from the chair.

"I'll see you later," Bellaire said, smiling at Maria and then at Rudy before leaving the room.

Moving close to Maria's bed, Rudy eyed the reclining chair, but did not sit on it. Not yet.

"May I?" Rudy asked Maria.

"You may," replied Maria in a serious tone, which was clearly feigned.

Rudy picked up on this, but just smiled as he gazed at the small sliding desk in front of Maria. It was neatly arranged. Coloring supplies were placed in one of the corners, two books stacked next to them. On the opposite corner was the framed photo of Maria and Billy. Rudy tried not to stare, but he couldn't help but look at the photo. It wasn't the idyllic farm setting or Billy that caught Rudy's attention; it was Maria. The slightly younger version Rudy saw in the photo had full, sun-kissed cheeks, a lively expression, and a beaming smile. It was clear she was happy there. Her bushy eyebrows seemed to mirror her dramatic eyes, and her long, dark brown hair fell in soft natural curls, framing her delicate face. Rudy was struck by what he saw in the picture. He knew, of course, that this horrible disease changed the children, but here in front of him was proof, with before and after photos of sorts. Regardless, her eyes, although changed by her illness, still had some sparkle, and her smile was still contagious.

"That's Billy. That's the farm," Maria pointed to a green and white house in the background of the photo. "And that's me before I turned into a white ball," she added, smiling while she rubbed the front of her head.

"White ball?" asked Rudy.

"The white ball," Maria said as if Rudy was missing the obvious.

"Cue ball. You mean the cue ball," Rudy said, and he couldn't help but laugh out loud. Realizing this could be viewed as derisive, Rudy immediately controlled his laughter and excused himself.

"Forgive me, that wasn't nice," Rudy said shyly.

"Why? Because I forgot the name?" Maria replied.

"No, calling you that is not okay," Rudy replied.

"Why? I like it," Maria said innocently.

"Who calls you that?" asked Rudy.

"Ray," Maria replied.

"Who's Ray?" asked Rudy, instantly realizing she meant Betances. "Wait, Betances calls you cue ball?"

"Um-hum," Maria replied.

"He didn't earlier," Rudy noted.

"No. He only calls me that when he reads to me or we talk when we are alone," Maria replied.

Rudy's head spun. Was this guy really mocking this sick little girl? What about the rest of the children? He was still wondering when Maria, who seemed to understand his concern, spoke.

"When he calls me that, he is being nice. He does it because he loves me," Maria said, the sparkle in her eye fading somewhat.

"Why do you say that?" Rudy asked.

Maria reached for the framed photo on her sliding desk, lovingly caressing the top of the frame and resting her thin little finger above the image of the boy standing next to her.

"Billy used to call me names, but he loves me. That's how I know," Maria replied, her gaze distant.

"What did he call you?" Rudy asked.

"Who, Billy?" Maria asked.

"Yeah," Rudy replied.

"Cow turd," Maria replied, giggling, her eyes shining again.

"Cow turd!" Rudy remarked.

Maria nodded, adding: "That was my favorite."

Their conversation was interrupted by Nurse Chen, who walked into the room with a small tray of food in her hands. She walked closer to Maria's bed, where she stood and waited for a second. Maria immediately gathered the things on her sliding desk and deftly placed them on the bed beside her. Chen then placed the tray on the sliding desk. Rudy noticed that what should be a dinner tray was mostly empty. The tray had a cup filled with a yellow liquid that looked like apple juice. Beside it was what looked like a covered soup bowl. Chen smiled at Maria as she uncovered the bowl, revealing its contents: three scoops of ice cream.

"Is that okay?" Chen asked.

Maria nodded, hiding a sly smile.

"Eat it all, and don't forget these," Chen added, placing a small transparent cup on her tray. Inside it were two small pills.

"Thank you," Maria replied.

"Call me if you need me," Chen said.

Chen was about to leave when she turned to Rudy.

"Doctor Dell, would you like some ice cream?" Chen asked.

"Thank you, but no," replied Rudy, surprised by her offer.

Chen smiled and left.

As Rudy watched Maria swallow the pills one at a time, he couldn't help but think about Betances's nickname. Despite initially finding it harsh, Rudy thought for a moment. He had to admit Maria's logic made sense, remembering all the name-calling he and his brother exchanged while growing up, not to mention how Rudy enjoyed torturing his brother with fake spiders. It was at that moment when his mind wandered into that memory that he sorely missed his brother.

"Do you have brothers or sisters?" asked Maria.

The question surprised Rudy. This was the second time Maria seemed to know what he was thinking. Was this girl reading his mind?

"Why do you ask?" Rudy asked.

Maria shrugged.

"I don't know, I just . . ." Maria looked down at her ice cream.

Rudy hated himself for forgetting he was dealing with a little girl. He wanted to tell her he was sorry, but decided against it.

"I have a younger brother," Rudy said in an upbeat manner.

That seemed to have the desired effect on Maria. She quickly gazed back at him and turned her head inquisitively.

"Did you call him names?" Maria asked.

"Yup. We both did, but I got him back," Rudy said.

Maria allowed her spoon to fall back into the ice cream bowl; her eyes shone more than they had before.

"What did you do?" Maria asked, excitement in her voice.

"Eat. You don't want the ice cream to melt," Rudy said.

"What?" Maria asked again.

"You can't tell him I told you; he would kill me. Promise?" Rudy said as he moved close to Maria and whispered, as if telling her a great secret. Her expression changed. She was clearly enjoying this.

"My brother is terrified of spiders," Rudy said, placing his index finger over his mouth.

"Really?" Maria asked. She, too, spoke in hushed tones, as if sharing a dark secret.

Rudy nodded an exaggerated nod before he continued.

"This one night, he was out partying with friends while I was studying very hard. The nerve," Rudy said, watching Maria's expression.

"Yeah," Maria replied, shaking her head.

"Well, it was late and he still hadn't come home, so I snuck into his room, raised the bed's covers, and filled the bed with plastic spiders. Then I replaced the covers," Rudy said, again raising his finger to his mouth.

Maria nodded, repeating the gesture.

"What happened?" she asked.

"I went back to my room and waited for him to come back," Rudy said.

"You didn't fall asleep?" a concerned Maria asked.

"Nope. Lots to study and I wanted to see what happened," Rudy said.

"What happened?" Maria said.

"When he finally arrived, it was well past midnight. I heard the door to his room open and he called my name," Rudy said.

"Why?" Maria asked.

"Sometimes I would hide in his room to scare him. I'm not proud of this," Rudy said. "Well, maybe a little."

Maria giggled.

"Then what happened?" she asked.

"Oh, he took so long. I heard him go to the bathroom and back to his room a hundred times, but I waited. You have to be patient with these things," Rudy said.

Maria nodded with a serious demeanor.

"Then, when I was least expecting it, it happened!" Rudy said.

"What?" Maria said, her eyes wide.

"The screams," Rudy said.

Maria cupped her hands over her mouth.

"Yes, he screamed like—" Rudy stopped and frowned for a moment before he continued. "Pardon the expression, but he screamed like a scared little girl."

Maria laughed loudly, and it struck Rudy that she had a great laugh.

"There's more," Rudy said.

"More?" Maria said, still laughing.

"Yup. He came out of the room, plastic spiders stuck all over his pajamas. He swatted at them with his hands, trying to get them off, and he kept screaming," Rudy said as he got up and swatted at his clothes while he jumped around the room.

Maria laughed even harder.

Rudy wasn't used to dealing with children and had dreaded the idea when he learned where he was going to spend the next few weeks. Surprisingly, he now found himself enjoying making the girl laugh. Rudy walked back to the chair and slumped down on it while Maria dried the tears off her face.

"But that's not all," Rudy said.

"No?" Maria asked.

"Nope. See my brother screamed so loudly—" Rudy said.

"Like a girl," Maria interrupted.

"Like a scared little girl, and I laughed so hard that we woke up our dad," Rudy said.

Maria's laughter came to an abrupt halt, concern on her face.

"What did he do?" Maria asked.

"Well, he came down to our rooms. It took a moment for him to understand what had happened, and when he did, he almost laughed," Rudy said.

"Really?" Maria asked.

"He had to. It was too funny. But he didn't. He looked at us and said that we were a couple of idiots. He then left, and I swear when he closed the door to his room I heard him laugh," Rudy said.

"What did your brother do?" Maria asked.

"Oh, he tried to catch me, but I ran into my room and closed the door. He banged the door a few times, but I told him I had more spiders with me and he left," Rudy said.

Maria laughed again.

Rudy smiled back, remembering the distant night clearly, and for a moment he missed his brother dearly.

"What's your brother's name?" Maria asked.

"Al," Rudy replied.

"Still afraid of spiders?" Maria asked.

"Terrified," Rudy replied.

Maria frowned as if she were thinking.

"If you try to scare me with plastic spiders, I think . . . yeah . . . I think I would be brave," Maria said resolutely.

"You would be, I'm sure," Rudy replied.

Rudy fought hard to keep his expression straight, affected by her comment. This little girl, who wondered if she would be brave, was dying, and she knew it. From what Rudy could see, she was the bravest person he had ever met.

CHAPTER 10

Rudy had spent quite some time speaking with Maria when Chen came into the room and told Maria it was her bedtime. Maria sulked as any child of that age would. Still reluctant to go to sleep, she finally acquiesced after some convincing.

"Let me get some things and I will keep you company until you fall asleep," Chen said.

"I'll stay," Rudy said.

Chen eyed Rudy inquisitively.

"I'm off in a few hours; you are not. You should get some sleep, Doctor Dell," Chen said.

"If I go to the on-call room, I won't go to sleep either. I'll just read my review book. Might as well do that here. Well, if Maria doesn't mind," Rudy said, looking at Maria.

"It's okay," Maria said.

"Fine," Chen said.

Rudy sat back and reached for his review book as he watched Chen leave. The room lights were off, but the small glass window on the door allowed enough light for him to read. Rudy flipped through the pages, coming to his bookmark. He began to read from this last marked position, but suddenly he came to halt and felt compelled to say something.

"Good night, Maria," Rudy said softly.

"Good night, Doctor Dell," Maria replied.

"You can call me Rudy," Rudy said.

"Okay, good night, Doctor Rudy," Maria replied.

"Just Rudy," Rudy chuckled. "Good night."

Rudy smiled silently before slowly turning back to his book, finding his place, and reading from where he had been before. It was then that Rudy realized he was behind in his reading. His original plan had him reading from sixty to a hundred pages a day, but that had been dependent on being on an easy rotation with lots of free time. If he wanted to keep up with his schedule, Rudy was going to have to take drastic measures. Without hesitation, Rudy sat forward on the chair and started to read, making annotations in a small notebook and fighting his own tiredness.

Rudy didn't know how long he had been reading non-stop when the door to Maria's room opened. Whoever opened the door did so slowly, careful to make sure not to wake up Maria. Turning his head when he heard the door, Rudy found Chen carrying a small basket. Rudy placed his small notebook inside his review book, marking the page. He noted the page before he closed the book, realized he had managed fifty-four pages short of his daily minimum. He would need to find some time and continue reading if he wanted to catch up with his planned schedule. So it was his intent to continue reading after morning rounds were over.

In order to keep from falling asleep as he read, Rudy had sat leaning forward in an uncomfortable position. This had managed to do the trick, but now as he got up, he paid the price. His back ached. Massaging his back as he moved away from the chair, Rudy suddenly felt an urge to rub his eyes, which burned noticeably.

"Did you get any sleep?" Chen asked in a low voice.

Rudy shook his head.

Taking a deep breath, Chen placed her small basket on the bed's sliding desk, which was now at the foot of the bed. Carefully, she slid it up closer to Maria. From the basket she produced a set of gloves, which she handed to Rudy.

"Put those on," Chen ordered. "When nature calls, listen. When you can, eat. When there's time to sleep, do." Chen added.

Rudy nodded, shuffling his hands as he put on the gloves. He then turned to Chen, feeling a slight headache.

"Here, add that to her IV, but keep the drip closed," said Chen as she handed Rudy a small saline piggy-bag.

Following her instructions, Rudy swiftly did, turning to Chen only to find her handing him a second piggy bag, which he also added to Maria's IV. Curious, Rudy read the handwritten script on both bags.

"Steroids and diphenhydramine," Rudy read. His drowsiness made it difficult for him to understand why she was getting these medications. It took a moment for him to realize these were in case of an allergic reaction. Chen most likely had read his momentary confusion as she explained: "In case she has a reaction from the transfusion."

Rudy nodded, kicking himself.

"I'll be right back," Chen said.

Not long after, Chen returned with the transfusion bag, which she expertly set up. Before starting the transfusion, Chen made sure Maria's vital sign telemetry was running properly. Then she turned to Rudy.

"She needs to be awake. We need to know if she feels well during the transfusion," Chen said.

"I'll do it," Rudy offered.

"Let me," Chen said as she delicately reached for Maria's shoulder. "Maria, honey."

Maria moved and spoke in a sleepy tone. "What?" she asked.

"It's time, honey," Chen said softly.

"Oh, okay, I'm ready," Maria replied.

Slowly Maria got up and rubbed her eyes with the backs of her hands. The gesture impressed Rudy, for it was so childlike, so innocent, yet Maria seemed so nonchalant about a blood transfusion. She turned and gazed at the blood, which was now flowing down the tube, then at Rudy, whom she didn't seem to expect to find.

"Good morning, Rudy," Maria said, making a point of enunciating his name.

"Morning," Rudy replied.

"You are sleepy," Maria noted, smiling.

"Yes, I am," Rudy said.

"I told you to get some rest," Chen said, turning to Maria. "Feeling okay?"

"Um-hum," Maria replied.

Chen turned and looked at the monitor above Maria's bed.

"Everything seems fine," Chen noted, turning to Rudy. "Dell, you need to watch her vitals, and watch her closely."

"I will," Rudy replied.

"Closely," Chen stressed.

"I will!" Rudy replied.

"Maria, I'll see you later, honey," Chen said before leaving.

As soon as Chen left the room, Rudy moved close to Maria, hunching over her and coming within inches of her face.

"What are you doing?" asked Maria nervously.

"Watching you close, very close. Like Chen said," replied Rudy, making a face.

Maria giggled.

Rudy made a face of exaggerated contempt.

"Hey, don't laugh! I'm watching you. This is serious work," Rudy replied before joining her in laughter.

Maria then laughed harder, which made her look less like the sick little girl she was and more like a normal kid. Rudy didn't understand why, but he thoroughly enjoyed making Maria laugh. He then sat in the chair, making an exaggerated point of the motion. When he did, he sat on his review book. He reached for it and stared at it for a second as he considered reading some more, but decided against it, quickly tossing the book aside.

"Neither of us can go to sleep. So what do you want to do?" Rudy asked.

Maria shrugged.

Noticing the books on her nightstand, Rudy offered to read her something.

"No, it will make me sleepy," Maria said.

"TV?" asked Rudy.

Maria nodded with enthusiasm.

"Okay, let's see what we can find at four in the morning," Rudy said.

Rudy reached for the remote and searched channel after channel, but he could not find anything that appealed to Maria until he came to an infomercial.

"Wait, that, leave that!" Maria said.

"What, the car wax commercial?" Rudy asked.

"Yes, he is crazy," Maria said joyfully.

Rudy took a deep breath and watched as an overexcited spokesman set fire to the hood of a car and cleaned it up afterwards with a towel. From the spokesman's hyperkinetic and hyper-verbal mannerisms, Rudy was sure the guy had to be taking some sort of stimulants.

"Who watches this?" he asked himself in a whisper. Then he turned and saw Maria laughing as she watched the excited antics of the spokesman.

"You like him?" Rudy asked.

"He's so funny," Maria said.

Rudy turned back to the TV. After watching the spokesman perform several crazy antics to showcase the product, Rudy had to admit the man was, in fact, funny. As was the audience's exaggerated reaction to the spectacle. Every single one of them seemed awed by the car wax's miracle properties. Satisfied, Rudy lay back in the chair and laughed with Maria until the infomercial was over.

"What now?" Rudy asked.

Maria shrugged.

"Let's see what we can find," Rudy said as he started running down the channels.

"Rudy," Maria called, apprehension in her voice.

"Feeling okay?" asked Rudy, becoming worried.

"Yes. It's just . . ." Maria said coyly.

"What?" Rudy asked.

"Do you think it's going to work?" Maria asked, her eyes pleading.

"The transfusion?" Rudy asked.

"Um-hum," Maria replied.

"We hope so, but we won't know until we check the labs," Rudy said.

"I know, but do you think it will help me go to Disneyland?" Maria asked hope in her voice.

Rudy was at a loss. How could they have told her this, knowing that it was a Hail Mary at best?

"I know it's a secret, but . . ." Maria replied.

Rudy smiled painfully. It was not his face that ached but his spirit. He desperately wanted to assure her. He didn't want to give the girl false hope, but he didn't want to shatter what little hope she had left either. Rudy didn't know what he could say. Then, as if sensing Rudy's dilemma, Maria spoke, releasing him from the burden of her question.

"What else did you do to your brother?" Maria asked, smiling softly.

Rudy understood what she had just done and was so very thankful. He couldn't help but admire the little girl in front of him, so aware of her fate, and yet so brave in the face of it. Rudy had never before come face to face with such a situation, he wondered how he would face his own mortality and mostly he wondered if he could ever be worthy enough to be her doctor.

CHAPTER 11

Rudy still had some difficulty speaking after Maria's inquiry regarding the upcoming trip. With some effort, he managed to relate another tale of sibling torture, which delighted Maria and lightened the mood somewhat. After that, Rudy continued scrolling through the channels and found a shark documentary, which Maria seemed more than eager to watch.

Still, Rudy could not help but think of Maria's simple dream, to have one day, just one day, in the park. He recalled the many times his parents had taken him and his brother to Disneyland, so often that it had become ordinary to him. So much so that once he had complained about having to spend the weekend there because of visiting relatives. Rudy felt more than a little shame that he had found the trips his parents worked so hard to provide mundane and common, especially when the girl besides him dreamed of nothing else.

It was a quarter past six when Mike showed up at Maria's room.

"How's everyone doing?" Mike asked.

Rudy watched as Maria gave Mike a thumbs-up.

He replied: "All's well."

"You don't look too hot, bud," answered Mike.

"Spent the night studying," Rudy said.

"Nerd!"

The commentary seemed to surprise Maria, who turned and stared at Rudy. He studied her for a second, realizing she fought to hold back a smile. Rudy then shrugged, nodding in acceptance, which made Maria smile broadly and giggle.

"Okay, okay, laugh it up," Rudy added.

"We are ready to do morning rounds," Mike said.

"I'll be there. Could you send someone to keep an eye on this one?" Rudy pointed suspiciously at Maria. "She is a troublemaker."

Maria smiled mischievously.

"Ramirez is on her way," Mike replied before he left.

Rudy turned and reached for his review book, which had fallen between the cushions of the reclining chair. He folded it, the notebook still inside, and somehow managed to fit it in one of his coat's pockets.

"I have to go, but I'll check on you before I leave for home," Rudy replied, unsure why he offered to do that.

"Okay," Maria replied cheerfully. "Will you tell me more stories about your brother? They were really funny," she added.

Rudy sighed. It was her cheerful disposition which so impressed him. She was so ill, so weak, her fate all but sealed, but her mood never wavered.

"Yes," Rudy said.

Ramirez came in carrying a small tray, which she placed on the sliding desk in front of Maria.

"Doctor Dell, everyone is waiting for you," Ramirez said.

"Bye, Maria," Rudy said.

"See you later?" Maria asked.

"You bet," Rudy replied.

As he left the room, Nurse Hathaway moved past him carrying a small red container. Maria's transfusion had been completed more than an hour ago, so Rudy knew Hathaway was going to draw the first blood sample.

"Good morning, Dell," remarked Hathaway as she passed Rudy.

"Morning," Rudy replied before heading down the hall.

Rudy found Betances, Mike, and Andropov standing in front of the nurses' station going over a chart.

"Good morning," said Rudy, announcing his arrival.

Everyone greeted Rudy, including Betances, but he just nodded to acknowledge him.

"Any problems last night?" asked Andropov.

"Checked on everyone before ten; quiet night after that," replied Rudy.

"Maria's transfusion went as planned?" Andropov asked.

"No problems. She complained of chills about an hour after the transfusion, but there was no fever, nothing more," Rudy explained.

"Hathaway is drawing the first samples as we speak, but we won't really know until tonight," Andropov observed.

"Let's go," Betances ordered.

The group went about rounds as usual, Johansson following along. Everything went as expected until they came to Tim's room.

"Any word?" asked Andropov.

Betances shook his head.

"All the pathologists know the case well and what's at stake, so they are making sure," Andropov said.

Betances nodded gravely.

"Let's move on to Maria's room. I'll sit down with Tim after," Betances said.

The group moved past the doors and into the isolation area, while Johansson stayed behind and began the day's work.

"Suit up," said Andropov.

Betances glared at him, but everyone got the protective gowns on.

"Good morning, Maria. How are you feeling?" asked Betances.

This surprised Rudy. Although he hadn't noticed yesterday, today he realized Betances never greeted the patient upon entering the room, always waiting for the fellow, residents, nurses, or students to fall in first, but not with Maria.

"Great. I feel great," Maria replied, despite her complexion telling otherwise.

Slowly and carefully, Betances sat at the foot of her bed, making sure not to move or disturb the bed. Rudy watched and considered asking why but decided not to, at least for now. Beside them, Ramirez sat on the reclining chair but did not speak.

"Well," Betances said before silently mouthing "cue ball." Maria giggled at this and gazed at Rudy as if letting him in on a secret. Betances seemed to pick up on this and glared at Rudy before he continued.

"Now we wait. Hathaway or Ramirez will get blood every four hours and we'll see. Is that okay with you?" Betances asked.

"Um-hum," Maria replied.

"Excellent," Betances exclaimed before turning to Rudy. "How was the new help?"

Maria laughed.

"He's okay," Maria said with a sideways smirk.

"You let me know if you have any trouble with him. We could have him reassigned—toilet duty," Betances said.

"Yes, sir," Maria said, trying to sound menacing.

"Good. Now if you'll excuse us, we are going to talk behind your back for a while," Betances said.

The group came out of Maria's room and into the small hall past the isolation doors. Betances motioned everyone to stop while they were still inside.

"Andropov, check her labs; keep me posted. Dell, Davenport, go home now," Betances said as he walked past the doors and inside Tim's room.

"Come on, buddy. You look like crap," Mike told Rudy.

It was then that Rudy realized that Mike wasn't supposed to be there. It was Saturday, so Mike wasn't required to come in unless he was on call, and he wasn't.

"What are you doing here?" Rudy asked. "It's Saturday."

"Forgot what day it was. When I realized I didn't have to be here, I was already in the parking lot," Mike said. "C'mon, I'll buy you breakfast."

"Okay, give me a minute," Rudy said.

He then turned back and headed inside Maria's room.

"Hey, Maria," Rudy said cheerfully.

"Hey, Rudy," Maria replied.

She glanced quickly at Ramirez, then back at Rudy.

"Are my labs okay?" Maria asked, a hopeful expression on her face.

"Still not back," Rudy replied.

"Oh, okay," Maria said, disappointed.

"Don't worry, honey. The important results are the ones from this afternoon and tomorrow," Ramirez said.

"Okay," Maria said.

"So, I'm going home. I'll see you on Monday," Rudy said.

"You're not coming tomorrow?" Maria asked.

"No, it's Sunday. Only the doctors and students on call come in," Rudy explained.

"Oh," Maria said.

Rudy could swear there was a note of mild disappointment in her voice. He didn't know what to say, so he said the first thing that popped into his mind.

"Mike will be here," Rudy said reassuringly.

"Oh, okay," Maria said, her tone still disappointed.

Remembering the transfusion, Rudy wanted to wish her luck, but didn't know how to say it. He felt a yearning to make her smile.

"The Force will be with you," Rudy said, smiling.

Maria frowned, turning her head. She clearly didn't get the quote.

"*Star Wars?*" Rudy asked.

"I don't understand," Maria replied shyly.

"You've never seen *Star Wars*?" Rudy asked.

Maria shook her head.

"We need to change that. On Monday," Rudy said.

"Monday?" Maria asked.

"I'll show you what *Star Wars* is on Monday. It is the best," Rudy said, sounding excited without meaning to.

"Okay," Maria said, picking up on Rudy's excitement. "Does *Star Wars* have any spiders?" she asked.

Rudy laughed. "Ha. No, but it's pretty great anyway. I'll see you Monday."

"Bye," Maria replied.

CHAPTER 12

Mike insisted on going to breakfast. Rudy was so tired he didn't argue, and just followed Mike's car. It was so early that they drove through a mostly empty city, allowing Rudy to drive almost unconsciously. Almost, as his mind was not completely empty. Rudy could not shake the disappointed look on Maria's face when he told her he wasn't working on Sunday. He wondered if he should just show up for the morning round, say hi, and then leave. Thinking this surprised him, as he knew he should be using the day to catch up on his studies. He still couldn't understand why he had been so taken by Maria. His thoughts were interrupted as they arrived at their destination.

The restaurant was a hot spot, but it was so early they managed to find parking in the nearby streets. Finding a table, on the other hand, would have proved difficult for most people, as the place was packed with a long line outside and probably booked for most of the day. Of course Rudy was not surprised when they were shown to their table as soon as they walked in. Rudy had learned that no matter where they went, Mike always had a reservation.

It was there, when they finally sat at the table, that the exhaustion caught up to Rudy.

"You need coffee," Mike commented.

"Coke, Diet Coke," replied Rudy.

"You heard the man," Mike said, turning to the server at their side.

Startled, Rudy turned to see a server whom he hadn't noticed before. This made Rudy finally acknowledge how tired he was.

"Diet Coke? How can you drink that so early?" Mike asked.

"Never went to sleep. So technically it's very late. Did we order any food?" Rudy asked.

"I did. You were out of it," Mike replied.

"Thanks, I still am," Rudy replied.

"Rough night?" Mike asked.

"Just kept reading. Before I knew it, it was time to work again," Rudy replied.

"Keeping up with your schedule?" Mike asked.

Rudy nodded before he downed his cold drink.

"Why? You are a shoo-in. Everyone knows you'll get in to your first choice for residency. They want you. All you need is to pass that Step Two. You don't even need to ace it. Hell, I'm sure you'll get in even if you fail," Mike said.

"It's not that," Rudy said as he signaled the server for a refill.

"Then?" Mike asked.

"I have to be the best," Rudy replied.

"Why so competitive? Who cares?" Mike asked.

"What the hell?" asked Rudy.

"There are more important things than school standings, my friend," Mike replied in a caring tone.

Rudy took a deep breath; he didn't want to get into this. Mike had drilled him about this during their surgery rotation a few weeks prior, and Rudy had no desire to revisit the conversation. Rudy understood Mike was concerned about his well-being, but Mike didn't get it; no one did. Mike would get into whatever residency he wanted. After all, he was a Davenport. Rudy wasn't rich or connected, so he had to stay on top. He had to keep his standing. He had to excel. It was his nature, and he wasn't going to give up. To just pass the test wasn't an option.

"Here you go." The server set the plates in front of them.

Rudy stared as his plate. There was a big piece of avocado on it. He hated avocado.

"Is everything to your liking?" the server asked.

"Perfect," Mike replied.

Rudy just nodded.

"Let me know if you need anything," the server said before leaving.

As soon as she left, Rudy reached for the avocado and placed it on his bread dish, pushing it far from his plate, then looked around to make sure no one saw him. Mike laughed at the calculated gesture, but Rudy just ignored him. He took the first bite of food. It was hot and tasty, but Rudy noticed he wasn't that hungry. Realizing this surprised him, as he hadn't had much food the day before and he usually had more than a healthy appetite. After a few more bites, he pushed the plate aside and sat back.

"That's all you are having?" Mike asked.

"Not really hungry," Rudy replied.

"But you are always hungry," Mike said, concern in his voice.

"Too tired to eat," Rudy replied.

After raising an eyebrow, Mike stood up. "Get some rest. We have plans tonight and you need to rest," he said.

"Plans tonight? No," Rudy said.

"Yes," Mike replied.

"What?" Rudy demanded.

"Julia is having a small press event and we are invited," Mike said.

"You go. She's your friend. I need to rest," Rudy said.

"We are both going because she's *our* friend. You have all day to rest," Mike said forcefully.

"But—" Rudy managed.

"No excuses. If you don't go, you'll just wake up late in the afternoon and study. You have to live a little. Besides, Julia invited you personally. Not attending would be poor etiquette," Mike said.

"Alright. I'll be there," Rudy replied, sulking.

"Poor Rudy. A fourth-year medical student, top of his class, and now invited by his friend, the model, to a private party full of her friends, more models," Mike grimaced as he said this. "It's just dreadful, the hardships. If you were a girl they could turn your life into a Lifetime movie."

"Jerk," Rudy said.

"Go home, get some rest, be there by eight," Mike said.

***

Rudy was dead tired as he drove back to his apartment; he was now on automatic pilot and mostly unaware of his surroundings. When he was a few blocks from home, something called his attention. He turned his gaze as he drove, and noticed he had just passed a video store. Unable to pinpoint why, Rudy felt the urge to go there. So as soon as he could, he made a U-turn and drove back to the store.

The store had just opened and was mostly empty, except for the employees who went on about their work. Rudy walked around the store in a daze. He had no idea what he was doing there, but he felt the need to keep walking around. Then, as he turned a corner, he remembered.

There in front of him was a large cardboard display full of videotapes from the recently released *Star Wars* video trilogy. Smiling as he shook his head in disbelief, he reached for the small box and headed for the register.

Soon after, he was back on the road and on his way home, the box containing the three videotapes on the passenger seat next to him. Again he thought about going to the hospital on Sunday morning. He could give Maria the movies and then leave. He also considered asking Mike to give her the videos, but no, he wanted to be the one that gave them to her.

Rudy suddenly found himself at his apartment. He was so tired that he decided not to argue with his body. He would go to sleep for a while. Once rested, his mind would be clearer. One thing was sure—he was not going to any party tonight. Rudy walked into his living room, sat on the couch for a moment, and collapsed.

***

Startled, Rudy woke to loud music. He sat up and noticed Mike sitting on a chair across from him, stereo remote control in hand. As soon as Rudy sat up, the stereo's volume decreased.

"Good morning," exclaimed Mike. "It's seven. You have thirty minutes to get ready."

"What's going on?" asked a confused Rudy.

"I have known you for four years. I know when you are planning to bail," Mike said.

"Shit," Rudy said.

"Get ready. By the way, I'll drive. I need to get back early; I'm on call tomorrow. So you'll have an excuse to leave early as well," Mike said.

A few minutes later, Rudy was sitting next to Mike as he drove them to the private event. While they moved down the city's streets, Rudy scanned his surroundings, which felt distant and foreign. It struck him as peculiar, for he knew the area well. He also felt uneasy. He blamed it all on his lack of sleep. It felt odd, Rudy had been on call before—bad ones, with far longer hours and more work—and had never felt quite like this afterwards. Rudy tried in vain to understand his current state as he rested his elbow on the car's center armrest. It was then that he realized that there was something strange about the car. Rudy had climbed into what he had believed was a Jeep, which was a little out of character for Mike, who almost always drove sports cars. But now Rudy realized he was in a Mercedes Benz.

"Mike, where the hell are we?" Rudy asked.

"What? You know where we are," Mike replied.

"No. The car!" Rudy said.

"Oh, took you long enough. It's a G Series. I thought you would like it," Mike said.

"A Mercedes jeep? I have never seen this before."

"It's a 1993, originally sold in Spain. My father saw it while he was there, bought it on the spot, and shipped it over. When he realized it was more like a Jeep and less like a luxury car, he lost interest. His current wife used it for a year or so and lost interest as well. It's been a few weeks since I moved it to my side of the garage," Mike explained.

Rudy turned to examine it more closely. It had two doors, four seats, and was wood and leather, but unlike most of the US Mercedes Rudy had seen, it was a stick shift. Beside the shift were the differential lockers and behind it, a second lever for the transfer case.

"This is very cool. Wait, it's not twenty-five years old. How did he get it approved for road use?" Rudy asked.

"What my father wants, he gets," Mike replied.

"I like it," Rudy nodded in approval.

"Thought you might."

Once at Julia's party, Mike kept his promise and left early. After all, he was on call the next morning. However, he neglected to tell Rudy. To Rudy's dismay, Mike just disappeared, leaving him stranded at the party. The funny thing was Rudy was having such a good time with Julia that it was close to midnight before he realized Mike had left.

As the party was winding down, Rudy tried to call a cab, but Julia insisted she would drive him home, which she did a few minutes later.

"Are you working tomorrow?" Julia asked Rudy.

"Not really," Rudy replied.

Julia smiled and kept her promise to take Rudy home. But she took the scenic route, taking Rudy to a few late nightspots, and lastly to an all-night Mexican takeout food truck.

The food was hot, fresh, and delicious, and Rudy ate more than his share, even going back for thirds. As before, he forgot to ask for the avocado on the side. So when he picked up his order and sat down next to Julia, he glanced at her quickly, wondering if he should pick out the avocado from his tacos.

"I have seen you take out the avocado twice before, and I have eaten it twice before. Aren't you going to do it again?" Julia asked.

Rudy smiled and quickly removed the avocado bits using a plastic fork, placing them on a small plate beside his tacos. Julia reached for the plate.

"I don't get you. You had raw octopus at the party, but not this?" Julia asked.

"I don't do eggplant either." Rudy shrugged.

"You are one weird little man," Julia said as she laughed.

Rudy couldn't help but stare at her blue eyes and her compelling smile. He had noticed before that she had the slightest hint of a gummy smile, and now he thought it made her look beautiful.

After their late night—or rather early morning—snack, Julia finally drove him home. By his estimation, it was past three in the morning when he finally made it back. The long night, coupled with Friday's lack of sleep, managed to knock Rudy down as soon as he came home.

Rudy awoke slowly. It was light outside and he didn't know the time, but at least he knew it was Sunday. Well, he hoped it was still Sunday. Quickly checking his wristwatch, Rudy confirmed it was in fact Sunday, and past five o'clock.

Now sitting on the side of the bed, Rudy noticed he was still wearing his suit. Body aching and still feeling exhausted, he took off his jacket and headed to the kitchen. There he reached into the fridge and produced a can of cola and a couple of slices of cold pizza. Rudy was about to place the slices in the oven, but he just took a bite of the cold pizza instead. He ate and frustration set in; he had lost most of the day. Deciding that if he wanted to get any reading done he needed a shower, Rudy headed into the bathroom.

Shower done and coffee in hand, Rudy sat down to read. Only a few pages in, he fell asleep on the couch, but just for a moment. There was no way he could get any studying done, and Rudy knew it. He stood up and tossed the review book on the dining table. The book landed next to a bag on the table—the bag from the video store.

"*Star Wars,*" Rudy said in a low voice.

He then sat down, wondering how Maria was doing. He hoped she was okay. All of a sudden, he didn't care about not being able to get any studying done. Rudy was on call tomorrow. He could do as he did on Friday and study at night while he kept Maria company.

CHAPTER 13

It was quite early that Monday morning, and having arrived earlier than expected, Rudy decided to start setting up for rounds. Mike, who seemed to come out of nowhere, greeted Rudy, surprising him.

"Morning."

"Shit, you almost gave me a heart attack. You left me stranded at Julia's thing," Rudy said with indignation.

"I'm sure it was torture having tacos with her," Mike said with more than a little condescension in his tone.

Rudy smiled. Clearly Mike had kept tabs on him, and he *did* have a good time, so he changed the subject.

"I went to the on-call room, but you weren't there," he said.

"I was around. Got up early," Mike replied.

"Sure. Why don't we get set up for rounds?" said Rudy, eyeing Mike with some suspicion.

What was Mike really up to? Rudy wondered if Mike had some sort of relationship with someone in the hospital. Rules discouraged things like that, but it was not unheard of; in fact, it happened all the time. Still, Mike? Rudy had met several of Mike's female friends, but Mike had never referred to them as more than friends. If he ever had a girlfriend, or at least a friend with benefits, Rudy hadn't known about them. Mike kept his personal life close to his chest, but Rudy spent enough time with him to know he was not a player, and Rudy had never seen him flirt with coworkers or fellow students. But stranger things had happened.

"I'll print out the labs," Mike added.

"Thanks," Rudy replied.

They were so engrossed by their preparations that they didn't notice Andropov arrive about half an hour later.

"My, aren't you two industrious!" Andropov remarked.

His comment was so bizarre and foreign for him that Nurse Ramirez turned her head, frowning in his direction. Mike stared as well, while a confused Rudy looked at all of them in turn.

Shaking his head, Andropov smirked.

"Children, children," Andropov shook his head before he continued. "I'll use small words from now on. Are we ready?"

"Five minutes," Mike replied.

As Rudy hurried to help Mike finish setting up, he gazed at Andropov, who was placing a few calls. A few minutes later the group went on to start their unofficial rounds. They were almost halfway through when Betances showed up, somewhat earlier than usual.

"Anything?" he asked.

Andropov shook his head; he wore a grave expression that told Rudy something was wrong. Reaching into his pocket, Andropov produced a set of folded pages, which he handed to Betances. Unfolding them, Betances scanned the pages one by one, doing so several times before he finally spoke.

"Seen her yet?" Betances asked.

"No," Andropov replied.

Rudy watched as Betances scanned the pages once more, as if hoping to find something he hadn't before. Allowing himself a deep sigh, Betances handed the pages back to Andropov.

"Get that on her chart," Betances said, anger in his voice.

"It was worth a shot," Andropov said.

"Yeah," Betances said in a low growl. "Come get me before you see Tim."

Rudy watched as Betances moved past them and into the nurses' lounge, his usual expressionless face showing what Rudy could have sworn was a mix of anger and frustration.

"Are those Maria's lab results?" Rudy asked.

Andropov nodded.

"We waited until the labs set late last night. We knew then, but weren't going to spoil her night," Andropov said as he handed Rudy the results. Reading them twice, Rudy felt his heart sink. He gazed back at Andropov, who shook his head.

"Nothing," Rudy said, feeling almost out of breath.

"The cancer is too aggressive. It literally burned through the transfusion," Andropov said.

Mike grimaced as he exhaled.

"He wants to be there when we see Tim," Andropov said.

"More bad news?" Rudy asked.

"I hope not. As far as I know, we haven't heard from the pathologists yet," Andropov replied.

"Mike?" Rudy asked.

"No news yesterday," Mike replied in a somber voice.

"Let's move on," Andropov said as he motioned everyone to follow him.

They were coming to Tim's room when Betances joined them from out of nowhere. Apparently he had been following their progress the whole time. Moving ahead of everyone, Betances opened the door and motioned everyone inside before he entered the room.

"Hey, champ, good morning," Andropov said, announcing the group.

As everyone exchanged greetings, Rudy noticed Tim turn his gaze to Betances, who stood there silently. Seeming to suspect something was up, Tim moved closer to the edge of the bed. Betances moved closer, meeting him. With an ominous stare, Betances knelt beside the bed and spoke in hushed tones with Tim, who listened intently and nodded.

Betances got up and placed his hand on Tim's shoulder as he addressed Tim's parents.

"I heard from the last pathologist this morning. He called me on my way here," Betances announced.

Rudy felt nauseous; more bad news.

"They are all negative," Betances said.

Tim's mother covered her mouth as her face distorted with a thousand different emotions. Tim's father stood up, placed his hands over his wife's shoulders, and moved past her, reaching for his boy with extended arms. With a huge grin, Tim reached back and embraced his father. Chris returned the hug, laughing and crying as he spoke loudly.

"My boy, my boy, my boy is okay," he continued.

Tim's mother moved past everyone and hugged Betances tightly, then Mike, Andropov, and Rudy before joining her husband and son. There was a long solemn moment as the group watched the small family rejoice. Rudy knew there was no urge to leave. Time stood still, for they reveled in the good news as well.

Rudy found himself smiling. The weight he had felt upon hearing that Betances had finally heard from the pathologists lessened as Betances announced the good news. He turned to see Tim, whose face was flushed and teary as he returned the hugs from his parents. A few minutes later, Betances addressed the group again.

"I'm sorry it took so long, but we needed to be sure. We did every test in the book, and some not in the book, including some DNA markers," Betances said.

"Thank you," replied both parents.

"No need. He finished our experimental protocol two days ago, so he's good to go. Dell, get his discharge papers ready. Tim, get packing. I want you out of here!" Betances said.

After a few more hugs, the group came out into the long hallway, just before the doors to isolation.

"Dell, go discharge them. Andropov, Davenport, straighten out the ward. I'll go talk to Maria," Betances said.

The elation that Rudy had been feeling upon hearing about Tim extinguished itself the moment Betances reminded everyone of the bad news he was about to deliver to Maria. Feeling again disheartened, Rudy walked back to the nurses' station and absently filled out all the paperwork in order to discharge Tim. He was about done when Tim was wheeled up to the nurses' station, followed by his parents.

"You are all set," Rudy said. "Hey, what's with the wheelchair?"

"Discharged patients must be wheeled out of the hospital for their own safety," replied Nurse Johansson.

"Right. Tell you what; do you mind if I wheel him out?" Rudy asked. "If that's okay with everyone." Rudy turned to Tim's parents. "I would like Tim to tell me more about those Yankees."

"Deal," replied Tim with excitement. Chris nodded with a huge grin and still watery eyes.

As he wheeled Tim down, Rudy was given a not-too-abridged history of the New York Yankees. Once on the elevator, the rest of the passengers smiled as Tim continued his discussion, which was not too far from a doctoral dissertation. Regardless, Tim was delighted with the attention he got.

When they finally made it to the first floor, Rudy offered to wait with Tim by the curb so his parents could get their cars. Since they had been taking shifts, they had two cars at the hospital. While they waited, Rudy got down at eye level with Tim so he could speak with him.

"I'm so very glad you are okay, buddy," Rudy said.

"Me too. I don't want my parents to worry so much. I know it makes them sad," Tim replied.

This was not the first time Rudy had noticed the children worried more about their parents and how they were affected by their children's illnesses. But it was the first time he had seen it firsthand, and thus the commentary struck Rudy hard. That Tim wasn't worried about himself as much as he worried about his parents made Rudy ashamed as he recalled all the times he had felt sorry for himself. While he reflected on this, Tim's parents drove up.

"Come on, buddy," Rudy said as he pushed Tim closer to the first car. Tim reached into his backpack.

"Here!" said Tim, handing Rudy a baseball card, encased in a small transparent plastic envelope.

"What's this?" asked Rudy as he turned the card in his hand.

"Roberto Clemente Walker. Pittsburgh Pirates," Tim said.

"Not a Yankee?" Rudy asked.

"No," Tim said, nodding, "but a great player."

"I can't take this," Rudy said.

"It's a gift; you have to accept it. Read about him. He reminds me of you," Tim said.

"Me? I'm no athlete," replied Rudy, laughing.

"Not that. He liked to help people, like you," Tim said as he smiled.

Rudy felt his chest tighten with the words, thinking that he wasn't worthy of this gift or this kid's admiration. Rudy managed a difficult thank-you before helping Tim's parents get everything inside their cars. Now strapped in the back seat of the car, Tim called Rudy over.

"What's up?" Rudy asked.

"I love baseball, but . . ." Tim said, gazing quickly at his father who was climbing in the driver's seat, "I want to help people, like you all do. I think I want to be a doctor," Tim said in a hushed tone.

Taken aback, Rudy watched silently as Tim pulled the door closed and waved goodbye.

CHAPTER 14

Rudy hurried back upstairs to find Betances sending Andropov and Mike to check on the day's consults. Upon seeing Rudy come through the doors, Betances sent him after them.

It had been some time since Betances had them paged back to the ward. Andropov was finishing up a bone marrow biopsy and completed the work calmly before heading back. It was about an hour past lunch when Mike, Rudy, and Andropov made it back into the oncology ward. As they walked past the double doors, Rudy spotted Betances sitting behind the nurses' station counter. The large man was reading a book, but met Rudy's gaze. He immediately closed the book, but as almost always, remained expressionless.

"Anything?" Betances asked.

"Not much," Andropov said, handing Betances a copy of the consults.

Rudy watched as Betances went over every single consult, shuffling the papers back and forth for some time.

"I agree. Maybe you are being overcautious with that last one. I agree; prep for a bone marrow biopsy," Betances said as he handed the consults back to Andropov.

"It's already done. I was in the middle of it when you paged us. We headed back in a hurry. I still have to write up the note," Andropov replied.

Betances nodded, turning to Mike and Rudy.

"Discharges done?" Betances asked.

"All three," Mike replied.

Rudy nodded silently, still affected by Tim's words.

"We sent three healthy kids home," Andropov said, but Betances cut him off.

"How many consults left?" asked Betances.

"Three," Rudy replied.

Betances stood up and joined the rest of the group, motioning them to move. Andropov turned and led the way, with Betances following close behind. Mike and Rudy moved to follow, but Betances turned before they did.

"Stay here, finish up, and leave," Betances said, turning quickly and walking away.

Rudy and Mike were surprised for a moment, but walked back to the ward without a word. It was a few minutes before Rudy managed to speak.

"He's affected. I didn't think he could be," Rudy said.

"I don't know, I think it's more frustration. He doesn't like to lose," Mike said.

"Who does?" Rudy said.

"You two are more alike than you think," Mike said.

Rudy had wondered about that, but his personal motivations had always been the same. Rudy had to be the best. He had never cared about anything else. Now these patients, these children, had made him question his mindset, his motivations. Rudy was still lost in thought when Mike interrupted him.

"There's really nothing else to do. With the discharges, most of the work is done. Come on, let's have lunch," Mike said.

"I'm on call," Rudy replied.

"Right. Let's go down to the cafeteria before I leave," Mike said.

Rudy wasn't feeling particularly hungry, but he followed Mike down anyway.

After a quick lunch of insipid hospital food, Mike left Rudy back in the ward. It was still early, and from what Betances had said, Rudy didn't think there was going to be afternoon rounds, at least not academic rounds. Deciding that this would be a great opportunity for him to catch up on his studying, Rudy went inside the on-call room to get his review book. Reaching inside his bag, Rudy quickly found the review book, but he unexpectedly also found the videotapes he had gotten for Maria. The eventful morning had made him forget all about them. Placing the book on the bed, Rudy lifted the tapes, silently reading the three titles. He then reached for his book, pocketed it, and left the on-call room with the videotapes in hand.

Walking past the door to the isolation area, Rudy expertly put on the protective gown, slippers, and hat. He was surprised how in less than a week, donning and wearing the protective clothing had become so familiar. After knocking softly, Rudy went into Maria's room.

Inside, Rudy found Maria on her bed. She seemed asleep, with her back to the reclining chair. Nurse Hathaway sat in the chair reading to her. She did so softly, so as to not to disturb her if she was in fact asleep, but not so low that the words wouldn't reach her if she was awake. Hathaway nodded as Rudy moved closer, but continued reading until she seemed to come to the end of a chapter.

"Maria, you have a visitor," Hathaway said softly.

Slowly Maria turned, meeting Rudy's gaze. She forced a smile, but Rudy noticed her expression was different. Unlike before, her eyes lacked their shine, and her skin was ashen. Rudy was sure she must have looked like this before, but it was now somehow more noticeable. Then there were the lines—deep lines—in Maria's face, lines that had no business being on a child's face.

Rudy had walked in resolutely; he would give the girl the tapes, maybe get one going on the machine, and go study. Now he wasn't sure what to do, but he was quite sure he would get no reading done. His mind and his heart weren't up to it, and he couldn't leave her.

"What's that, Doctor Dell?" asked Hathaway, as if trying to move Rudy along.

Rudy looked down at his hands, seeing the tapes which somehow he had forgotten. Silently he raised the tapes and showed Maria.

"*Star Wars*, the full saga," Rudy said, trying to sound excited. "You said you've never seen it. It's for you."

"Seriously?" Maria asked, some excitement creeping into her voice.

"Yeah. I love *Star Wars*. I'm sure you will too," Rudy said, now managing to sound more convincing.

"Can we watch them?" Maria asked, turning to Hathaway and then to Rudy.

"Sure, honey," replied Hathaway as she got up from the chair.

Maria then turned back to Rudy, her expression somewhat softer now. "Will you watch with me?" she asked Rudy.

"Try and stop me," Rudy replied.

Suddenly Rudy remembered the book in his pocket and that he was behind in his reading. But after seeing how Maria's demeanor changed when he agreed to watch the movie with her, Rudy decided he didn't care much about the test.

Struggling to free the tapes, Rudy fought with the plastic shrink-wrap around the movies. He made a show of it, which made Maria giggle. He was glad that she did, thinking he had at least accomplished that. Hathaway was at the door ready to leave, but suddenly turned to say something and was interrupted by Maria.

"Nurse Hathaway," Maria said, hesitating before continuing. "Are you going to Disney with the other kids?"

"Yes," Hathaway answered in a low voice.

Maria tried to smile, but the corners of her mouth shook momentarily as several silent tears ran down her cheek. She took a deep breath, which turned into a sad whimper. But she did not allow more than that to show, forcing a smile instead. Then she spoke with a sad, trembling voice.

"Are all the kids going?" she asked.

"Yes, honey. It's just you are too weak to go," Hathaway replied with deep regret in her voice.

"It's okay, I'm happy they can go," Maria replied.

Hathaway nodded silently.

"Could you get me a bunny? It doesn't have to be a big one," Maria said with pleading eyes.

Hathaway looked confused for a second, then a smile of recognition spread across her face.

"Honey, I'll get you a great one," the nurse replied, clearly fighting to keep from crying.

Maria's eyes lit up. "Thank you," she said.

"Maybe next time, we'll take that trip together," Hathaway replied, fighting her emotions.

Maria nodded and smiled, but the lines in her face and her expression gave her away. Maria knew differently. She knew it was a compassionate lie.

After what must have been a difficult moment, Hathaway managed to speak. "Movies are no fun without candy. How about some ice cream? Rocky Road?" Hathaway asked.

Maria pouted as she shrugged.

"Don't worry, honey. I'll bring medicine so you don't get sick," Hathaway added.

Maria nodded.

"Dell? Ice cream?" Hathaway asked.

The question surprised Rudy, who caught Hathaway's gaze. Her intent was clear; he had to say yes.

"Yes," he replied, despite having lost his appetite.

"I'll be right back," Hathaway said before leaving.

Then Rudy caught a fleeting glimpse of Hathaway as she moved past the door. She raised a shaking hand to her mouth, silently crying as she walked away.

After placing the tape on the machine and pressing the large play button, Rudy moved the reclining chair close to Maria's bed. While the now-running videotape showed the pre-movie previews, Rudy sat, feeling a small jab in his side. Surprised, Rudy moved and found the rolled review book in his pocket. Without hesitation, he pulled it out, allowing it to fall to the floor. Still waiting for the movie to start, Rudy's attention was called to the book Hathaway had been reading.

"May I?" Rudy asked Maria, pointing to the book.

"Um-hum," Maria replied.

Rudy picked up the book and read the title aloud. "*The Little Prince.*"

"It's my favorite book," Maria said with longing in her voice.

"I have never read it," Rudy said. "Maybe I can read it with you."

Maria nodded silently.

The deep silence that fell between them was abruptly broken by a fanfare of trumpets that signaled the beginning of *Star Wars.*

The spectacle of flying ships, talking robots, and heroes fighting had Maria sitting up. Rudy watched as Maria absently ate her ice cream, some dripping over her pajamas. Rudy couldn't help but smile himself as he noticed Maria smiling— the smile he remembered from a few days back, the smile that made her eyes regain some of their lost shine. Her amazed expression reminded Rudy of how it was to be a kid, innocent to the world and in the presence of magic.

CHAPTER 15

It was already early evening. They had to stop a few times, but Maria and Rudy managed to finish *The Empire Strikes Back* before a nurse came in looking for Rudy.

"Doctor Dell, we need you to help us with something," Chen said.

This was the code they used in front of the patients, so Rudy knew that something was wrong. He was also quite sure all the children had picked up on it. In the little time Rudy had spent here, he had learned that these children had become quite adept at picking up on things when they went wrong, even when their parents didn't. Thinking hard, Rudy had to concede how strong these children really were. Like warriors, they had learned to lick their wounds and accept their fate with dignity, wearing their best faces for the benefit of all of those around them. He wondered if anyone else around here saw this. Why patronize the children? For all they were going through, they deserved honesty. Betances clearly understood this. Then it hit him. The codes, the secrecy, it was for the benefit of the adults. It had to be. How could the staff believe that they were somehow sparing the children from these horrors they all knew too well? Or maybe they were desperately trying to spare themselves.

"What's wrong?" asked Maria, tears running freely down her face.

Alarmed by the tears, Chen rushed to Maria's side.

"What's wrong, honey?" Chen said, alarm in her voice.

"Nothing." Maria wiped the tears off her face.

"But you're crying," Chen insisted.

"It's nothing," Maria replied, smiling.

"Maria, please tell me what's wrong." Chen came close to the bed. She then sat at the edge of Maria's bed, carefully, as everyone did, so as not to disturb her.

"Han's frozen. They took him away," Maria said, again wiping fresh tears from her face.

Chen frowned, for a moment clearly lost. She looked around the room and then at Rudy in an apparent attempt to figure out what was happening to Maria.

"Who's Han?" Chen said as her eyes narrowed.

"Han Solo," Maria said.

Chen's eyes widened and her face contorted. Rudy saw it clearly. She was angry and trying to hide it.

"Doctor Dell, Nurse Bellaire is waiting for you. Please go and help her. I'll keep Maria company," Chen said in a calm but sinister voice.

"Rudy," called Maria as he was about to leave.

Rudy turned, looking past Chen straight to Maria.

"Will you come back to watch the next one?" Maria asked.

Chen glared at Rudy.

"Definitely, as soon as I can," Rudy said.

Still wearing the protective gown, Rudy ran down the long hall to where Bellaire waited for him. Rudy made it to the main nurses' station. He was out of breath, but he made it.

"What's wrong?" Rudy asked.

"Megan. She's been running a fever," Bellaire said.

"She had her last chemo three days ago?" Rudy asked.

"Yes," Bellaire said, handing him Megan's chart.

Rudy checked her temperature and the medications given. He could see that over the last four hours, Megan had experienced a fast rise in body temperature. He then checked the medications given by the nursing staff and the little to no effect these were having. He quickly checked the labs, looking for cell counts, but the last samples had been taken four hours ago.

"We need to run some cell counts," Rudy said.

Bellaire reached for the chart and flipped to the orders page.

"Go ahead and sign the order. We took the liberty of drawing blood a few minutes ago. Smith is at the lab waiting for the results. We also called for an infectious disease consult," Bellaire said.

"Excellent, let's go check on her," Rudy said as he signed the orders.

Rudy quickly examined Megan. He was most concerned with hidden infections, so he looked for everything, including ingrown toenails, something often overlooked but that his surgery rotations had taught him to look for.

"How are you feeling, Megan?" Rudy asked.

"Cold. My head hurts a lot," Megan said.

Megan spoke in a low voice. She was rather slow, which was very unlike her.

"Are you sleepy?" asked Bellaire.

Megan nodded slowly.

But her mannerisms told Rudy she was not sleepy but rather lethargic.

"We can't wait for the infectious disease fellow to get here. Bellaire, set everything up for blood cultures, and get a urine sample kit. We need a urine culture as well," Rudy said.

"Shouldn't we wait for the consult?" Bellaire asked.

"Go get the supplies now!" Rudy ordered.

Bellaire hesitated a moment but ran out of the room. Rudy turned to Megan and Bruce.

"The fever could be from the treatment, but we need to make sure it's not an infection. So I need to get some blood from you, Megan. Is that okay?"

Megan nodded slowly.

Rudy then gazed at her father, looking for his silent approval. Bruce nodded before he spoke.

"Please do everything you can," Bruce replied.

Rudy nodded, trying to be as reassuring as possible.

Not five minutes later, Bellaire was back with a cart full of small glass jars. Rudy had done this often enough that he expertly set up everything. Bellaire seemed to approve, dutifully assisting Rudy, whatever misgivings she seemed to have washed away. Remembering Megan's knowledge of vascular anatomy, Rudy decided to ask her where to draw blood from, not only to humor her, but to make her feel a part of what was happening to her. Megan silently pointed as she had before, and Rudy went about cleaning the area with iodide and alcohol. He then set up the system he had used countless times before during his surgery rotations. In a moment, all the glass jars were filled as needed. He then cleaned the puncture wound and applied pressure so it would stop bleeding, carefully placing a bandage over the wound.

"You okay?" Rudy asked Megan.

Megan nodded slowly.

"One more thing, Megan. I need you to help Bellaire get a urine sample. You think we can take you to the bathroom?" Rudy asked.

Megan nodded almost imperceptibly.

"Bellaire," Rudy said.

Bellaire moved closer to the bed and, with help from Bruce, moved Megan to the bathroom in order to perform a clean catch urine sample for culture. A few minutes later, the trio came back out and slowly got Megan back to bed. Bellaire then turned and walked back to the bathroom, a small sealed plastic cup in hand.

"Excellent, place it there with the blood samples," Rudy said, pointing to the small cart.

"As soon as Smith gets back, I'll deliver these to the lab," Bellaire said.

"How's her temperature?" asked Rudy.

"I'll check," Bellaire reached for a thermometer.

Everyone waited, but Bellaire's expression said it all. Suddenly, an out-of-breath Smith walked into the room, a crumpled paper in her right hand. As soon as she saw Rudy, she handed him the paper. Rudy scanned the results, nodding.

"Neutropenic fever. We need to start antibiotics fast," Rudy said. "Bruce, I need to go do some calculations for the antibiotics, and when we get the cultures back we might need to change those, but it's imperative we start as soon as possible. Is that okay?"

Bruce just nodded, his lips pressed together tightly as he gently caressed Megan's hair.

"I'll be right back," Rudy promised, suddenly having an idea. "Bruce, it's not standard therapy and it may not do anything, but a shower may help lower her temperature and make her feel a bit better."

"Yeah, my mom used to do that," Bruce said.

"Bellaire, help them. I'll call someone to get the cultures to the lab," Rudy said.

"I'll take those down and run right back," Smith said, reaching for the cart and hurrying out of the room.

"I'll be right back," Rudy said as he left the room.

Once at the nurses' station, Rudy reached for the therapeutic manual and the antibiotic manual, both of which were always at the station. If he remembered correctly, he should start therapy with a single broad-spectrum antibiotic aimed at gram-negative bacteria. Rudy searched the books, finding the best alternative. He then followed with the task of calculating the antibiotic dosage for Megan's weight. He was still working the numbers when he heard someone panting across from him.

"I'm back," Smith said.

"That was fast," Rudy said as he finished his calculations.

"I'm a runner," Smith said. "What else do you need me to do?"

"Let's start this antibiotic," Rudy said, turning the chart around so Smith could read the orders.

"Right away," Smith said, running behind the nurses' station.

"Get some acetaminophen suppositories as well," Rudy added.

While Smith prepared the antibiotic drip, Rudy wrote an order for a chest X-ray. He made the call to radiology to have them send a tech with a portable X-ray machine, adding that he needed it done as soon as possible. He could have just written the order and had the nurses follow through, but there was no reason to wait, and anything he could do to help the nurses would help Megan. Rudy then asked to talk to the radiologist on call and explained the situation.

"Done," Smith said.

Without a word, Rudy and Smith walked back into the room. They found Megan back in bed, wearing different pajamas and shivering.

"Her temperature went down. Not much, but it's down," Bellaire informed Rudy.

"I feel cold. Is that okay?" Megan asked.

From her voice, Rudy could tell she was a bit more alert.

"You have a fever. It could be from the medicines they gave you or an infection. We are going to start you on some antibiotics now," Rudy said, pointing to Smith, who was already adding the small bag of antibiotics to Megan's IV. After that, Smith reached for a small cup beside Megan's bed.

"Honey, I have to give you some suppositories for your fever," Smith said.

Megan sulked as she turned on her side. Clearly this was not the first time for her. Nor for Smith, who inserted the suppositories in seconds.

"Okay, we wait," Rudy said, trying to think what else to do, knowing that for now the only thing they could do was wait and watch her. The doors to the room suddenly opened, and a burly man in green scrubs walked in pulling a large wheeled machine.

"Megan?" the burly man asked.

Megan slowly raised her left arm.

"Perfect, where's Dad or Mom?" the burly man asked.

"Here!" said Bruce.

"Perfect. Take this vest and put it on. Everyone else out," the burly man said.

Rudy, Bellaire, and Smith came out of the room, walking back to the nurses' station, where Smith returned Megan's chart, looking at the orders page.

"When did you order the X-ray?" Smith asked.

"While you prepared the antibiotic," Rudy said.

"Who called them?" Smith asked.

"I did. You guys were busy. I talked to the radiologist. He promised to send the tech quickly," Rudy said.

Bellaire and Smith exchanged looks for a moment before turning to Rudy.

"That was good thinking, Doc," Bellaire said.

"We're done. You can go back in," announced the burly man as he dragged the portable X-ray machine out of the room. "I'm taking the film directly to Doctor Gonzales. She will call you as soon as I give her the film."

"Thanks," replied Rudy.

Smith and Bellaire went back to the room. Rudy was about to follow them in when the infectious disease fellow showed up—a Doctor Geller. Rudy gave her a rundown of the case and what they had done so far.

"Any oral thrush?" Geller asked.

"None that I could find," Rudy said.

"Let me examine her," Geller said.

"Follow me," Rudy said, walking to Megan's room.

With the help of Smith and Bellaire, Doctor Geller performed a thorough exam, after which she addressed Bruce and Megan.

"The team here did everything we needed to do. Doctor Dell started the right antibiotics; now we wait. I'll probably start her on other antibiotics and antifungals in the next few days; that will all depend on the cultures. As we get results in, we may change the treatments. I'll be checking on you tomorrow," Geller turned to Rudy. "Page me if anything changes."

"I will, thank you," Rudy said.

Geller excused herself and left the room. Without thinking, Rudy went after her.

"Doctor Geller, one moment," Rudy called behind her.

"Yes?" Geller answered, turning.

"She's supposed to leave for Disneyland on Friday. Will she make it?" Rudy asked.

Geller frowned, looking inquisitively at Rudy. "You should know. Aren't you a fellow?" Geller asked.

"No. I'm a med student, fourth year," Rudy replied.

"Then who did all the cultures and the antibiotic calculations?" Geller asked.

"I did," Rudy said.

"Where did you learn to?" Geller asked.

"During my last clerkship," Rudy replied.

Geller nodded. "Good. Saved us some time and got the ball rolling fast. The oncology fellow is here every third or fourth night. The rest of the time a senior pediatric resident is on call and takes care of anything that happens here after hours. He probably wouldn't have done all this, and would have waited for me to get here. You did good, but how did you know about neutropenic fever?" Geller asked.

"I read about it. I was studying for the USMLE," Rudy replied.

"That's quite more advanced than the boards. Anyway, good for you and good for Megan," Geller said.

"Will she make it?" Rudy asked.

"I'm sorry, I don't think so. Even if all the cultures come back negative and she doesn't deteriorate, she still needs to get at least seven days of antibiotics, and she won't complete that by Friday," Geller said.

"Could she take the last few days orally?" Rudy asked.

Geller took a long, deep breath. Rudy watched her, hoping she understood what this trip meant, and why he was asking.

"Tell you what. If all goes well, you sell it to Betances and I'll try to sell it to my program director. How's that?" Geller said.

"Thank you. It means the world to her," Rudy said, again surprising himself.

CHAPTER 16

Rudy spent the rest of the night and early morning checking on Megan. Her chest X-ray was normal, as was the rest of her lab work. Well, at least within normal limits if he took into account her condition. It was a little past three in the morning when her temperature finally went down enough that it was within safe levels. Despite that, Rudy kept tabs on her for another hour just to make sure.

"Doctor Dell, she's stable. You have done more than enough. Please go get some sleep. We'll come get you if there's any change," Bellaire said.

"Yeah, yeah. I think I'll take you up on that," Rudy said, getting up from behind the nurses' station. As he did, he felt the weight of his exhaustion fall hard on him. It had been quite a long and stressful night. Rudy went into the small on-call room and made sure his alarm clock was set to go off at six thirty. It was somewhat late if he wanted to check on everybody before the rest of his team arrived, but he desperately needed the rest. He then sat on the small, hard bed, falling asleep even before his head met the hollow pillow.

***

A distant repetitive sound grew closer and louder. Rudy turned to see the alarm clock. It was six thirty. Knowing he didn't have much time, he jumped out of bed. Betances would arrive in less than thirty minutes. If he hurried, Rudy might just have enough time to be ready for the morning rounds. He tried in vain to straighten his coat and scrubs, but after sleeping in them, it was useless. They begged to be thrown into a wash. Rudy noticed a fresh set of scrubs on the small desk beside the door. Thinking he was pressed for time, he decided against changing. Coming out of the small room, Rudy ran into one of the nurses.

"Wait, go change. I'll get you some coffee," Ramirez said.

"I'm late. I have to get things in order before Betances gets here," Rudy replied, trying to walk past her.

Ramirez took ahold of Rudy's arm, pulling him around the corner that led behind the nurses' station. To his dismay, Rudy saw Betances hunching over a chart.

"Go change. I'll get you some coffee," Ramirez insisted.

"No, I have to," Rudy said as he tried to walk to the nurses' station. Betances was already there, Rudy was late; he didn't want to make things worse.

"Doctor Dell," Ramirez said as she blocked Rudy's way.

Rudy glared at Ramirez, and for a moment he was at a loss. He didn't know what to do, nor how to deal with her, when a resounding voice solved the dilemma.

"Dell, go change. Ramirez, make that two coffees please," Betances said.

"Yes, Doctor Betances," Ramirez said, moving away from Rudy.

With a yielding sigh, Rudy turned, walking back into the call room where he changed. Taking but a moment, he rushed out wearing fresh scrubs. He moved over to Betances, who was still hunched over the patient chart. Looking over Betances's shoulder, Rudy managed to read the name on the chart. It was Megan's. Betances flipped over the pages, writing orders every so often.

"Sit," Betances ordered.

Rudy sat as Ramirez handed him a cup of coffee. Without thinking, he drank the coffee. He wasn't surprised that after his long night, the hot liquid felt so comforting. He was, however, surprised at just how good it was. Unconsciously, he looked down at the cup, trying to figure out why it tasted so different, so great.

"Not bad?" Betances asked.

Rudy nodded.

"Somehow you have fallen on Ramirez's good graces and you get the good coffee. Pray it lasts," Betances said.

"What's in it?" Rudy asked.

Betances turned to Rudy. "How would I know?"

Rudy hated himself for asking. He was sure it was his exhausted state that made him ask stupid questions. Betances got up, making a motion with his right hand. Rudy understood, following close behind with Nurse Hathaway in tow. Betances and Rudy visited the few patients left in their care. As Rudy expected, they left Megan for last. Well, almost last, as they hadn't seen Maria yet. Rudy was standing with Betances outside Megan's room when Andropov and Mike showed up. Seeming to realize something was wrong, the two men hurried down, worried looks on their faces when they saw rounds had begun without them.

"Dell, give us a rundown of what happened last night," Betances said.

Rudy gave his best account of the events of the previous evening up until four, suddenly realizing he hadn't checked Megan's stats this morning. In a panic, Rudy reached for Megan's chart when Betances jumped in.

"Her vitals have remained stable since then. Temperature is still above normal, but far from danger. She does need close follow-up," Betances said. He then turned and walked inside Megan's room. Everyone followed close behind.

"Good morning," Bruce said.

"Good morning," Megan repeated.

Rudy walked past everyone, coming close to Megan, who looked more alert and more like her usual self.

"You look better," Rudy said.

Megan nodded. "I feel a bit better."

"That's excellent," Betances said. "Mind if I take a look at you?" he added.

Megan shook her head slowly.

"Good," Betances said a few moments later after having examined her.

Bruce sighed.

"I called the lab this morning. They promised me a preliminary on her cultures, but it is still too early. Nevertheless, if there's anything in the cultures today, we may better streamline treatment," Betances explained.

"Thank you," Bruce said, following with, "Thank you, Doctor Dell."

Betances glared at Rudy for a moment.

"He did a great job with Megan last night," Bruce added.

"Thank you, but there's no need," Rudy replied.

Betances gazed again at Rudy, who could swear the man was sizing him up.

"I'll come back later. Please call the nurses if anything changes," Betances said.

With everyone back at the nurses' station, Betances went over Maria's chart. Silently, he flipped over the most recent labs, turning to the orders section. Seeming to hesitate for a second, he quickly wrote down a set of orders. Rudy watched, seeing it was the same set of orders he had written every day. Pain and nausea medication to be given as needed, labs to be performed before lunch, then lastly to call him immediately if she deteriorated. Betances then turned and began to hand out assignments.

"Davenport, Andropov, start on the consults. I'll meet you in one hour at the third-floor lounge. We'll take it from there," Betances then turned to Rudy. "You are no good to me in your state. There's a new patient coming in today. Start the paperwork for protocol two." Betances pointed to a chart on the far corner of the nurses' station.

"Of course," Rudy replied as he watched Betances walk down to the isolation area. He was going to see Maria by himself.

Rudy reached for the chart, read the patient's history, and then drew a blank. What was protocol two? He turned to the two nurses behind him.

"Okay, I give up. What's protocol two?" Rudy asked.

Ramirez and Hathaway laughed.

"Smart boy. Usually residents stare at the chart for some time before they ask," Hathaway said.

Ramirez handed Rudy a set of papers. Rudy flipped the pages, almost ripping the staple out, which was loose on the worn paper. It was clearly a copy of a copy, as the words were partially washed out and distorted.

"Copy those orders, just like you have them there," Ramirez said.

"Thanks. Say, could I have some more of that killer coffee?" Rudy asked.

"Sure," Ramirez said.

Rudy had managed to write four lines of orders when Ramirez placed a large cup of coffee in front of him.

"Thanks," Rudy said as he took a large sip of the delicious liquid.

"What's in this?" Rudy asked.

"More calories than you can count," Hathaway replied, laughing.

"No, seriously," Rudy said as he continued writing orders.

"It's a secret recipe," Ramirez said, reaching for a small saline bag. "I'm going to give Megan her antibiotics."

"Secret recipe?" asked Rudy, but Ramirez was gone.

"Only Doctor Betances gets that coffee, and now you do too. That's high praise," Hathaway said, leaving to help Ramirez.

CHAPTER 17

Rudy was so tired that he had trouble copying the admission orders, having difficulty reading from the worn copies. After a few tries, he managed to get everything ready for the upcoming patient. Once he was done, Rudy walked back to the small on-call room. He gathered his things and was about to leave, but his mind drifted. Despite being exhausted, Rudy felt compelled to visit Maria before he left. He wanted to say goodbye just in case. He knew she was at her times' end. He didn't want to think about it, but he didn't want to learn she had passed and he hadn't said his last goodbye.

Placing his things behind the nurses' counter, Rudy moved down the hall. As he reached for Maria's door, it opened, revealing Nurse Johansson, who turned back and spoke to Maria, seemingly oblivious to Rudy.

"I'll be right back," Johansson said.

She then turned and glared at Rudy. If she was frightened by him she didn't say it, but her usually flat expression wavered momentarily, so Rudy knew that at the very least he had surprised her.

"I just came to say bye to Maria," Rudy said, trying to break the tension.

"Are you in a hurry?" Johansson asked.

"Not really," Rudy said.

"Could you stay with her for twenty minutes?" Johansson asked.

The peculiar request seemed curious to Rudy, who probed Johansson's flat expression, but it revealed nothing.

"Doctor Dell?" Johansson insisted.

Johansson's expression was still flat, but Rudy could swear there was a slight change in her tone, almost a silent plea.

"Sure," Rudy said.

"Thank you," Johansson said, forcing a smile.

Rudy nodded. He couldn't help but stare at Johansson's face before she left. The forced smile gave Rudy a chill; it was, in a word, frightening. Since arriving at the ward, and especially during the last few days, Rudy had come to know the nurses, getting a glimpse of each nurse's unique personality. Johansson was cold and calculating; not disrespectful, but almost like a robot. So her forced smile gave Rudy the impression that something not unlike a terminator had smiled at him, and then there was the request itself, which was quite odd. Regardless, he didn't mind. In truth, he wasn't in a hurry. Rudy was tired, but he wasn't sleepy. Soon he would be home finally getting some studying done.

Moving inside the room, Rudy found Maria busy drawing. She looked up upon hearing the door and smiled brightly.

"Hello," Maria said.

"Good morning," replied Rudy.

"Is Megan okay?" Maria asked.

"Yes, better," Rudy replied, knowing there was no point keeping what happened from her.

"That's good," Maria said.

As before, Rudy was struck by how concerned Maria was with the well-being of others, considering her own situation.

"Are you done?" Maria asked.

"Yeah, came to say goodbye, but decided to hang out with you for a while, if that's okay?" Rudy said, not mentioning Johansson's request.

"Could we finish *Star Wars*?" Maria asked, her eyes glowing with expectation.

"Well, I'm supposed to leave soon. Maybe we could watch it next time I'm on call," Rudy replied.

"Okay," replied Maria, disappointment in her voice and on her face.

"You know what? I just remembered Han is still frozen. I don't think he can wait two days," Rudy replied, walking up to the TV.

After turning on both the TV and video cassette player, Rudy reached for the last movie and placed it inside the player. He then sat back in the reclining chair next to Maria.

"Are you up for this?" Rudy asked.

Wearing a huge smile of excitement and clear gratitude, Maria nodded.

Once more, Rudy watched as the opening scroll moved up the TV. He turned to see Maria smiling, her face, pale as it was, showing anticipation. Rudy had wanted to get some studying done, but he decided to stay with Maria, realizing her request wasn't that of impetuous child, unable to wait. Maria knew her time was short. She might not be here in a couple of days. How could Rudy deny her this little precious time?

A few minutes into the film, Johansson walked into the room, speaking loudly. Rudy immediately shushed her.

"We are watching a movie," Rudy said in a low voice.

Johansson looked at the TV, then at the smiling Maria, who applauded when Luke first appeared, and then back at Rudy. Her eyes were inquisitive, allowing Rudy to read them well.

"You'll have to come back later," Rudy said.

Johansson smiled again, but this time it wasn't forced. Rudy was quite sure it was an authentic smile. Just before she left the room, Johansson faced Rudy and mouthed a silent thank-you. Despite the sincerity of the smile, her change in demeanor still gave Rudy the chills.

Turning back to the movie, Rudy smiled, thinking how great it was that Maria was able to enjoy these films for the first time. He remembered first seeing the movies as a kid with his family all those years ago. He was glad that he could give this to Maria. It was then that he was struck with a realization. In an unusual turn, he was not preoccupied with studying; his mind was not desperate to keep with some schedule. It felt foreign. It had been a long time since he had felt content and just focused on what he was doing, but just now, he did. Rudy again smiled at Maria, whose gaze was fixed on the TV, knowing he would rather be here than anywhere else.

The time flew while they watched the movie. Rudy felt silly, but he couldn't help but be moved. He hadn't seen the film in years, but it brought back fond memories. As for Maria, Rudy could see she, too, was moved. As the kid she was, Maria had applauded the hero's triumph. Now she was singing along with the Ewoks during the movie's finale. Suddenly she reached for Rudy and pointed at the screen as a robe-wearing Anakin appeared among the spirits of the Jedi.

"He was good, he was good," Maria said excitedly.

"Yes."

"And Luke and Leia, they are together, a family," Maria said while a tear ran down her cheek.

"I'm sorry, I'll turn it off," Rudy said, afraid he had made the girl sad.

"No, no. She loved Luke even when they were apart, even when she didn't know he was her brother." Maria reached for the framed photo next to her. "Like I love Billy, even if I can't tell him."

She returned the picture to its place, then reached for one of her books and flipped over to a marked page. Rudy watched as she read it before she handed him the book.

"Read," Maria said, pointing to a few underlined lines.

Rudy reached for the book and noted it was old and worn. But unlike an old discarded book, its pages were worn from repeated readings, for this book was clearly cherished.

"Read," Maria insisted.

Rudy nodded and read the text aloud.

"'It is only in the heart that one can see rightly; what is essential is invisible to the eye.'" Rudy read it again in silence, looking at Maria in turn.

"Luke and Leia loved each other, even if he didn't say it. Like I love my brother, even if I can't tell him," Maria said.

"Yes," Rudy replied as he turned the book over. "But I think this is more complex than that."

"No, it is simple. The little prince is a kid, like me," Maria added.

"The prince?" Rudy asked as he read the title of the book.

"*The Little Prince*, that's the book," Maria added.

"I don't know it," Rudy said apologetically.

Maria opened her eyes in clear astonishment.

Rudy flipped through the pages. As he came to the first page, there in a child's script was an inscription: *Property of Billy*.

Rudy showed Maria as he pointed to the script.

"It was Billy's book. He used to read it to me. When I got sick, he gave it to me," Maria replied with longing in her voice.

"Maybe I should read it when I have the time," Rudy said.

"You need to, before you forget how to be a kid," Maria said.

"What?" Rudy asked.

"It's something the prince says. You like the movies, so you still remember how to be a kid, but grown-ups forget. They forget to have fun, they wait to have fun," Maria said, her expression far away.

Without directly saying so, Maria had once again reminded Rudy of how little time she had left. She didn't say it outright, but he understood. She was clearly telling Rudy not to take his time for granted. Looking at Maria, Rudy was amazed by the wise little girl and her reverence for life. He handed Maria her book back, aware that it was a prized possession and a reminder of her brother.

"Billy sounds like a great guy," Rudy said absentmindedly.

"Um-hum," Maria said with a pained expression.

"I'm sorry, I shouldn't have brought it up," Rudy said.

"It's okay. I miss him so much," Maria said.

"I'm sure he misses you too," Rudy said.

Maria smiled with difficulty, clearly fighting the tears back. Rudy felt horrible for bringing the subject up.

"Could we watch the end again?" Maria asked. "I like the bears, and the song."

"Sure thing," replied Rudy as he walked over to rewind the tape. "You know, I have a friend who would be offended that you called them bears."

Maria frowned momentarily.

"They are bears—no wait, teddy bears—but my friend is obsessed with the movie. He wears *Star Wars* pajamas," Rudy said. He made a face, which seemed to have the desired effect, as Maria smiled.

"Oops, I rewound too much," Rudy said.

"It's okay, leave it," Maria said.

"You really liked the movies?" Rudy asked.

"Yes," Maria replied.

***

A few minutes later, Maria was again singing alone to the movie's finale when Mike walked into the room. He turned as he heard the music and looked at the TV, then back at Rudy.

"Really? You had to torture the poor girl?" Mike asked.

"She's never seen them," Rudy replied.

"I liked them," Maria said.

"I'm too late. He has you in his cult. You know he has *Star Wars* pajamas," Mike said loudly.

Wide-eyed, Maria stared at Rudy, clearly fighting to hold back a smile.

"You got me," Rudy replied, throwing his arms up in an exaggerated gesture.

Maria laughed a loud, honest laugh that filled the room.

Ramirez walked in carrying a tray of food, turning to the TV as she did.

"Is that the one with the teddy bears?" she asked.

Maria and Rudy exchanged glances and laughed together.

"What am I missing?" Ramirez asked.

"Nothing, Dell just got Maria into his *Star Wars* cult," Mike replied.

"Sure. Maria, could you make some room, honey?" Ramirez said as she placed the tray on the sliding desk. "Betances was looking for you," Ramirez added, pointing at Mike.

"Yeah," Mike replied. "C'mon, buddy, let's see what the boss wants."

"You'll be okay?" Rudy asked Maria.

Maria nodded.

"I'll be here," Ramirez said.

Walking out of the room and out into the hall, Mike turned to Rudy. "Go get some sleep. I'll pick you up at seven," he said.

"What?" Rudy asked.

"Pete's band is playing tonight at the strip. Julia will be there," Mike said.

"There's little point in me saying I don't feel like it," Rudy said.

"That's the spirit. See you at seven," Mike said before he left.

Rudy took a deep breath and headed down the hall, but he was struck with an idea, quickly turning back to the nurses' station. He reached for the phone and dialed a number from memory. After a few rings he was connected.

"Hey, Chuck, it's Rudy," Rudy said.

"Hey, buddy, is everything okay?" Chuck asked.

"I'm calling to ask for a favor. I need to find this boy. He was adopted about a year ago. His stepsister is in the hospital, and, well, I think it would mean the world to her if she could see him," Rudy said.

"That's a tall order. Come over; we'll have lunch. Get me everything you can on this boy and I'll see what I can do. No promises," Chuck said.

"Thanks," Rudy replied.

CHAPTER 18

Rudy drove straight to Chuck's office. After catching up, Rudy gave him all the information he managed to gather about Maria, Billy, and the family that had been fostering them at the farm. Once finished, and since Rudy didn't get to see much of Chuck these days, they went out for a late lunch, spending much of the afternoon reminiscing about college and high school. After that, Rudy drove straight home in hopes of having a productive night. But once in his apartment, his mind distant, his thoughts turned to Maria and the book she was reading. After a few minutes hesitation, Rudy reached for his car keys and headed for the door, determined to get a copy of the book for himself. Upon opening the door, Rudy was surprised to find Mike waiting for him.

"Where are you going?" Mike asked.

"Nowhere, just out," replied Rudy.

"The concert?" Mike asked.

"I forgot," Rudy said.

"I'll drive," Mike said.

"Man, I need to get some rest. I can't stay out all night," Rudy said.

"Take a cab back if you need to leave. You shouldn't be driving after last night, but we have to be there for Pete," Mike said.

"Exactly. I should get some sleep, not go out," Rudy said.

"You only live once," Mike added.

The comment reminded Rudy of Maria, and how her time was running short. He came to understand what she had said implicitly—enjoy your time.

"Seize the day," Mike said.

"Yeah," Rudy said.

**

They arrived at the club some minutes later. They walked inside through the back entrance, as their friend Pete had arranged. Once inside, Mike and Rudy were directed to the dressing room, where they met Pete, the band, and Julia, who waited with a friend. After exchanging greetings and a few casual conversations, Julia walked up to Rudy and offered him a glass of wine, which he accepted.

"Mike told me you had a rough night. I thought you would pass on the concert," Julia said.

"I almost did!" Rudy replied.

"I'm glad you didn't," Julia said, smiling.

Rudy couldn't help but stare at Julia's deep blue eyes and perfect cheekbones, still amazed that she was hanging out with him.

"What?" Julia asked, clearly noticing his stare and covering her nose subconsciously.

"Nothing, it's just . . ." Rudy managed.

"I know, my nose. Promise you'll fix it when you become a plastic surgeon," Julia said, slowly uncovering her face.

"What? No, don't change anything. You're stunning," Rudy said, surprising himself with the comment and feeling immediately embarrassed.

Julia smiled, perking up. As she did, Rudy swore she beamed.

"You really think so?" Julia asked.

"Well, yes. I'm sorry," Rudy said uncomfortably.

"Sorry for what?" Julia asked, surprise in her voice.

"I didn't want to sound like a creep. I'm not hitting on you," Rudy replied.

Julia laughed loudly, actually snorting, which made Rudy smile. She reached for Rudy's arm and led him to a long table at the back of the room.

"A piece of advice—a girl never tires of being told she's beautiful," Julia said.

"It's just . . . I didn't want to sound . . ." Rudy tried explaining, but he couldn't get the words out.

"I get it," Julia said, smiling. "In my line of work, you learn to tell the difference between the pervs, the dangerous people, and the nice guys."

"I can be dangerous," Rudy said, unable to believe he had just said that. What the hell was wrong with him?

"Sure. So, you know the dangerous ones try to convince you they are nice," Julia said. "You haven't touched your wine. Let's get you something else," she added as they reached the table.

"So, I'm a nice guy?" Rudy asked.

"I think so," Julia said.

"Mike?" Rudy asked.

"Definitely dangerous," Julia said.

"You know firsthand?" Rudy asked.

"Yes, in fact I think he left with Bianca," Julia said, scanning the room.

Rudy moved, scanning the room as well, seeing that both Mike and Bianca were not to be found.

"See?" Julia said.

"Point taken. You know more about Mike than I do," Rudy said.

"We are very close," Julia replied.

"Very close?" Rudy asked shyly.

"Doctor Dell, do you want to know if Mike and I were ever involved?" Julia asked.

Rudy didn't reply, unsure what to say, but Julia volunteered the information.

"No, he's more like family," she said reassuringly. "We have been friends since junior high, when I first came to the West Coast."

"How did you become friends?" Rudy asked.

"Why do you want to know?" Julia asked.

"He doesn't have that many friends. You know, when I first met him I really didn't like him," Rudy said.

"It was the same for me," Julia said.

"So?" Rudy insisted.

"When I first came here, I had this thick Southern accent. I was new at the school and some boys were making fun of the way I talked. I was crying, but they didn't care; the boys kept at it. Mike came out of nowhere and stood up for me. He even got in trouble," Julia said with a faraway look in her eye. "Friends ever since."

"Outcasts have to stick together," Rudy said.

"Yes. How do you know that?" Julia asked.

"He never mingles with the rest of our class. So I once asked him why he was friends with me," Rudy said.

Julia pulled Rudy's arm closer. "See? We are more alike than you think," she said.

Rudy smiled, still unable to believe that he was talking to a model whose photo was on magazine covers and actually having things in common with her.

"Let's go see Pete play," Julia said.

"I'll probably leave after the first set. I'm beat. Last night was brutal," Rudy said.

"I'll drive you," Julia said.

"I'll take a cab," Rudy said. "I don't want you to miss the show."

"I'll drive you. We can stop on the way for tacos from that all-night place and you can tell me about last night," Julia said, smiling.

Rudy nodded. He was actually looking forward to that.

CHAPTER 19

Rudy woke up dazed. His hearing was dull, making the alarm clock sound distant. Unlike most mornings, he got ready slowly, walking out of his room later than usual. He didn't have time for breakfast, so he reached inside his fridge for a Coke when a brown bag caught his attention. He didn't remember it. The bag felt substantial. Pulling it out, he peered inside and saw a large burrito from Julia's favorite all-night taco place. For a second, he had difficulty remembering, but then it came back to him. They left the club after the first set, and as promised, Julia drove him to the all-night taco place she loved. They had a quick bite and Julia drove Rudy home. He didn't remember buying the burrito. Regardless, it was a perfect breakfast, so he placed it in the microwave. It was then that he noticed a note inside the bag.

Figured you could use this, had a great time last night, Julia. Call me.

Flabbergasted, Rudy stared at the handwritten note. He still couldn't believe he was friends with Julia. Was she really interested? She seemed to be. His train of thought was interrupted by the beeping microwave, annoyingly announcing his food was ready.

Knowing he would be late, Rudy reached for the steaming burrito and his Coke and headed for his car. It wouldn't be the first time he would eat while driving. He was actually quite adept at it.

***

Rudy stood behind the nurses' station while Andropov gave him a rundown on the night's occurrences. Mike had arrived a few minutes before Rudy, and Andropov had sent him down to the lab to check on Megan's blood cultures. While they waited, Rudy helped Andropov load up the cart with supplies and patient charts. They had everything ready when Nurse Hathaway joined them.

"Andropov, Betances is on the line for you," Hathaway announced.

Andropov thanked her and walked over to the phone in the corner. It was then that Ramirez came in with several cups on a tray. She placed the tray on top of the nurses' station before addressing everyone.

"Coffee?" Ramirez asked.

"Thanks," replied Rudy, reaching for the cup nearest to him.

Ramirez caught him before he could reach for the cup.

"This one is yours," Ramirez said, handing Rudy one of the cups from the back.

Rudy accepted the cup, enthralled by the familiar smell of Ramirez's special coffee. Ramirez smiled, acknowledging his recognition.

"Where's Johansson?" asked Rudy, noticing she was nowhere to be seen and wondering if he should be worried.

"With Maria," replied Hathaway.

"Is everything okay?" Rudy asked.

Hathaway nodded, but her expression confirmed something for Rudy. It was clear that the nurses tried not to leave Maria alone, something he had realized when Johansson had asked him to keep her company. As if knowing what he was thinking, Hathaway broke the silence.

"She is all alone; too weak to walk and too sick to leave. We try to make sure she's never alone, especially at night."

Understanding that this was not part of their job description, Rudy had nothing but admiration for these nurses.

"You, too, have helped," Hathaway added.

If he had, it was not consciously, at least not initially. Rudy felt a rush of shame that he hadn't thought about it. Still, he had helped, unconsciously or not. Rudy's expression hardened and he considered saying something, but Hathaway interrupted him.

"You don't do things like this because it's expected of you, or because you are told to. You do them because someone needs them, because it makes their life that much better. Because it's the right thing to do, even if no one finds out. *Especially* if no one knows," Hathaway said.

Rudy's breath faltered. What he had done, if anything, he had done without meaning to.

"It doesn't have to be planned. You just do it, because"— Hathaway tapped her chest above her heart—"you feel it here."

Rudy felt out of breath, his mind conflicted.

"I have seen many students like you. They come through here, they survive, and they move on; no lasting impact, no scars. You seem different. I think this place will stay with you; it will scar you," Hathaway said, giving Rudy a caring look.

Rudy nodded. He didn't quite understand, but he felt it would be impolite to ask for clarification. The short silence that followed was broken by Andropov, who walked back, coffee in hand.

"Betances is with Davenport down at the lab, checking Megan's cultures. Let's get rounds started," Andropov said.

Rounds went without incident. Marcus, the seven-year-old boy admitted the day before, was away having a PET scan. Megan's temperatures were better but her cell counts were off, and her kidneys weren't functioning as they should. Before going into her room, Andropov turned to Rudy.

"Don't talk, just listen," Andropov said.

Uncertain, Rudy nodded as he followed Andropov inside Megan's room. There they found Bruce, Megan's father, reading to her. Uncharacteristically, Megan, lay in bed on her side. She stared at her father with her eyes half open. Her expression was flat, devoid of a smile, and her skin had turned a pallid gray. Upon noticing them, she gazed up and smiled softly. She tried to speak, but a low hello was all that she managed. Bruce stood up. His eyes showed he was eager for good news, but they had none to give him. Andropov's expression must have given him away, as Bruce's face darkened upon seeing it.

"Any news?" Bruce asked, his tone grim.

"Not yet. Doctor Betances is down at the lab waiting for results," Andropov said.

Bruce nodded as a worried look swept across his face. An uncomfortable silence followed. He seemed about to say something when a weak voice interrupted him.

"Don't worry, Daddy. I don't like it when you worry. It's going to be okay," Megan managed. She stretched her thin arms and motioned for her father. Managing a heartbreaking smile, Bruce reached for her hand.

"I'm sorry, honey, it's just—" Bruce stuttered. "I love you, honey."

"Me too, Daddy. Don't be sad. Everything is going to be okay," Megan added.

Bruce inhaled deeply, a thousand expressions hidden below his unconvincing smile. Rudy could tell the man was fighting a great personal turmoil and wondered if he himself could ever truly understand.

"Daddy, would you read to me some more?" Megan asked.

"Sure, honey, but the docs need to examine you," Bruce said.

"It will just take a minute. May I?" Andropov asked.

Megan nodded.

Andropov went about it quickly, smiling softly when he finished.

"All done. What are you reading?" Andropov asked.

"*The Lost World.* Megan loved *Jurassic Park.* It's the sequel," Bruce said.

"I loved the dinosaurs," Megan managed.

"They are very cool indeed," Andropov said.

Megan nodded as she closed her eyes.

"We'll get out of your hair," Andropov said.

Bruce, who had returned to the chair beside the bed, gave Andropov a pleading gaze.

Andropov nodded. Rudy understood Bruce's silent plea. As they left the room, Rudy heard Bruce reading to his daughter. Rudy drew a deep breath. He wasn't a religious man, but regardless, he recited a silent prayer for her.

Once out in the long corridor, Andropov moved behind the nurses' station and tapped the counter. Rudy sat next to him as he tried in vain to catch his breath. His head spun, trying to come to grips with what he had just witnessed.

"You understood what just happened?" asked Andropov.

Rudy nodded. "Megan was comforting her father," he said.

"I have never gotten used to it," Andropov said.

Rudy stared at him in amazement. Rudy had truly believed he alone had been affected, but Andropov was too. Rudy had held many expectations for this forced and unwanted clerkship. None had related to this—seeing a sick child, a dying child comfort his parents. There was no way to explain how brave and selfless these children could be. Rudy felt an admiration for these poor, outstanding children that he had never felt for anyone. If someone had told Rudy that these things happened, he would have not believed them. Witnessing it firsthand, he still couldn't understand the impact it had on him. There was a profound sorrow he could not describe in simple words. And for the first time in his life, he questioned his decision to become a doctor. For the first time in his life, he considered walking away from it all.

Rudy sat next to Andropov, who stared silently at the monitors. Rudy didn't speak, still reeling from the deep impressions left from what he had just witnessed. It felt like a painful stab that tore away a piece of him, leaving a deep wound. As he thought about it, he remembered Hathaway's words.

"I think this place will stay with you. It will scar you," Hathaway had told him.

Rudy now understood; he felt it. And he feared this would be the first of many scars.

CHAPTER 20

It was quite some time before any words were said, and Rudy was fine with that, until he suddenly remembered Maria. They hadn't seen her. Not knowing if enough time had passed, Rudy spoke up.

"Excuse me, Doctor Andropov. What about Maria?" Rudy asked.

Andropov stood up and turned to face Rudy.

"Dell," Andropov said, "last night was a rough night for her. If she's asleep, we won't wake her. We won't order any labs, not today."

"Is she okay?" replied Rudy with concern.

Andropov nodded.

"She has some good days and a lot of bad days. It's the road she's on," Andropov replied.

Andropov didn't say anything else, but he didn't have to. Rudy knew this to be true. They were about to go into isolation to check on Maria when Andropov's pager went off. Rudy watched as he read the message in silence.

"We need to go down to see a consult," Andropov said.

Rudy nodded.

"Dell, why don't you go check on Maria? I'll call you if I need any help," Andropov said.

"Sure," replied Rudy, thinking that Andropov seemed to need some time alone.

After Andropov left, Rudy walked into Maria's room. He did so carefully, making sure to make no noise, but to his surprise, Maria was already awake. Beside her, he saw Johansson working on a chart next to the bed. She immediately rose.

"I'll be back in a little while. Call me if you need anything," Johansson told Maria.

Johansson walked past Rudy, tilting her head as if to say something, which she didn't, but she didn't have to. By now, Rudy was in on it. The nurses kept a watch of sorts over Maria. Hathaway had confirmed as much. They made sure she spent as little time alone as possible. Thus he knew that if he left, he was supposed to notify one of them so they could keep the girl company. Rudy wondered if Mike was doing this as well and made a mental note to ask him.

Rudy turned to see a smiling Maria. She seemed somehow smaller. Her smile was frail, not forced, just not as alive as before. Her skin was ashen, her eyes sunken, and she looked thinner, if that was even possible.

"Good morning, Rudy," she said, her voice raspy and weary.

Rudy replied in kind as he sat next to her. It was then he noticed the stuffed toy she held tightly in her arms. He couldn't remember seeing it before. It certainly looked new. It was a stuffed animal of sorts, dark reddish-brown in color, bright and unfaded.

"Who's that?" Rudy asked.

Maria looked down at the toy, offering it for Rudy to see. Rudy reached for it, examining it carefully once he had it. In his hands, Rudy held a substantial stuffed rabbit, with expensive-feeling fake fur and detailed features. It looked as close to real as possible. Rudy turned the toy, looking for tags, but he found none. Then he came to the toy's right leg. There on one of the footpads, sewn in dark red stitching, was Maria's name. This was not only new, but custom-made.

"He was here in my bed when I woke up last night, when I felt sick," Maria said.

Rudy had heard about Betances doing things like this, so he guessed he had sent for the expensive-looking toy for Maria.

"It's a he?" asked Rudy as he handed the toy back to Maria.

"Yes, his name is Bunny, like my rabbit," Maria replied as she took back the rabbit and unconsciously caressed his head. The childish gesture impressed upon Rudy the realization that Maria, his dying patient, was just a little girl. He lost track of their conversation but found his place after a moment.

"Back at the farm you had a rabbit?" asked Rudy.

"Yes, no," Maria replied.

"Which is it?" asked Rudy.

"Back at the farm, Mrs. Miller had a vegetable garden near a big apple tree," Maria explained. "Almost every day, some rabbits would come and eat from it. We were supposed to chase them away, Billy and me. We would run screaming and the rabbits would jump away and run around. I chased them all over. It was fun. I think they played with me, but there was one who would stay, looking at me."

"He didn't run away?" asked Rudy.

"No, when I saw him I ran to him and he waited, twitching his nose. I think he was smiling at me, but he jumped away when I got close. He didn't run away. He hopped a few times and turned back, and he looked at me," Maria said emphatically.

"Did you catch him?" Rudy asked.

"No, he jumped away when I got close, and when all the other rabbits ran away, he would leave," Maria said.

"So what did you do?" asked Rudy.

"I chased the rabbits every day. They all jumped in circles; I'm sure they were playing with me. But the big brown rabbit always looked at me and waited. So one day, I went to the kitchen, I cut up an apple, and I put it in my pocket. Then I went down to chase the rabbits. I ran all around, but when I saw the big brown rabbit I stopped," Maria said.

"Did he take the bait?" Rudy asked.

"Not bait. I didn't want to catch him. I wanted to be his friend," Maria replied.

"That's what I meant," Rudy said, embarrassed.

"I walked very slowly. He didn't jump away. He just looked at me, twitching his button nose and turning his head side to side. When I came close, I put the apple slices in front of me and walked back. Slowly he moved, eating a few slices. After a few days he would let me pet him, but he would run away as soon as I did. I didn't chase him, so he stopped and turned, looking at me, always turning his head."

"I think he wanted to play with me; he wanted me to chase him. So I did, all over the farm. When I got tired and had to sit down—I think I was starting to get sick—he came back and let me pet him for a while. After that, he came every day looking for me, my brown bunny," Maria said, gazing down at the toy and hugging him tightly.

"Does he look like him?" Rudy asked.

"Um-hum," Maria nodded as she again embraced the big toy rabbit.

"He's beautiful," Rudy said, wondering what happened to her rabbit, but deciding not to ask her, fearing that he would draw up a painful memory. Unexpectedly, as if reading his mind, Maria explained.

"I played with Bunny for a long time, and one day he didn't show up anymore," Maria said.

Rudy nodded but didn't inquire, still afraid to make the girl sad.

"The others came. Billy and I chased them, but Bunny didn't come back. One day after chasing the rabbits, Billy showed me the moon. It was out, big and beautiful. He said that Bunny had jumped all the way up there," Maria said, a deep yearning in her expression.

Rudy smiled as he reached and carefully petted the toy rabbit.

"He's not going to bite me?" Rudy asked.

"Silly," Maria said with a shy smile.

"I know Billy was making fun of me, but that night he gave me *The Little Prince,*" Maria reached for the book on her nightstand, offering it to Rudy before she continued.

"He started reading it to me. The prince had a goat on his planet, so I asked Billy if Bunny was in the moon with a little prince. He said I had to keep chasing rabbits, and one day I would find Bunny again. Maybe he could come back from the moon and take me there to play, to be his princess," Maria said.

Rudy took a deep silent breath as he turned the weathered book in his hand.

"Would you read to me?" Maria asked shyly.

Rudy nodded, flipping the book open. He gazed at Maria, who held the toy rabbit tightly with a faraway look. Rudy felt himself sinking, realizing that this simple act meant the world to this poor girl. Rudy fought a foreign feeling. He felt overwhelmed, and for a second he struggled to hold back the tears. Rudy finally found some footing and read aloud.

"*Once when I was six years old . . .*'" Rudy began reading.

CHAPTER 21

Rudy had read several chapters when he noticed Maria had fallen asleep. He wasn't sure how long ago. He had kept reading, as he was rather intrigued by the story. Rudy closed the book and carefully placed it on the nightstand. Rudy then reached into his pocket for the board review book he was still carrying around. He opened it, searched for his last bookmark, and tried reading. For quite some time, he stared blankly at it, unable to read or concentrate. Rudy closed his book, admitting to himself it was useless. He then reclined in the chair and looked at Maria, who slept clutching the brown rabbit. She seemed more than tired; she seemed spent. Knowing what was to become of her, Rudy wondered if she was close. For an infinite moment, his mind fixed on Maria, all alone, and the image of Megan comforting her father.

These past years, Rudy had witnessed many things in hospitals all over, gruesome, unbelievable things, but Maria, Megan, Tim, and the other children had shown him a side of life, a side of his chosen profession, that was completely unexpected. Nothing he had seen before had shaken him so. He was still lost in thought when Johansson walked back into the room.

"They are looking for you," Johansson said.

Rising slowly, Rudy gazed at Maria, feeling a sense of loss as he was about to walk away from her. Johansson watched him as she sat on the chair next to the bed. Silently, she started to work on one of the charts she carried with her. Rudy turned back to Johansson but decided there was nothing to say. As if understanding, Johansson nodded grimly, which was unusual for her.

Rudy walked out and down the hall where Mike waited with Andropov. Betances was nowhere to be seen.

"Buddy, you don't look so hot. You okay?" Mike asked.

Rudy just looked at Mike for a second, trying to process the question. He searched for words, but he felt helpless, unsure what to say, or how to convey what he was feeling. In the end, he just shook his head.

"Good thing I'm the one on call today," Mike added.

Rudy wondered if he knew about Megan, if he had seen her comfort her dad, and if Mike had been as affected as he was.

Andropov seemed to be, at least to a degree. Rudy considered asking Mike, but by his demeanor, Rudy surmised he hadn't been. So, chasing the idea away, Rudy moved behind the counter and joined them.

"Any news on Megan's cultures?" Rudy asked.

Andropov frowned and shook his head.

"No, but with neutropenic fevers there's a high risk of infections, so empirical treatment continues. We will repeat cultures soon."

Rudy knew as much but hoped for good news.

"Betances left to resolve a personal matter. We still need to go see two consults. Follow me," Andropov added.

***

It was past three when they made it back to the ward. Rudy went over to the computer and printed out all the new lab results, but there was nothing regarding Megan's cultures.

"I'll do a quick round with Davenport before leaving. Dell, go home. You're on call tomorrow and you look like you need some rest," Andropov said.

"You look like hell," Mike added.

Rudy felt like it, but he wasn't tired. It was something else entirely. Andropov's demeanor mimicked Rudy's, so he suspected that Andropov was at least as affected as he was and needed to get out of here as much as he did. Rudy was sure that was the reason Andropov was dismissing him before afternoon rounds.

"Have a good call," Rudy told Mike.

"Thanks, buddy," replied Mike as he and Andropov walked down the ward's long corridor.

Rudy watched them for a second and turned, intent on saying goodbye to Maria, but before he could, Hathaway called him over to the counter.

"She's still sleeping. Johansson is still with her. Go get some rest," Hathaway said.

"I will as soon as I get some notes done," Rudy said.

Still feeling restless, Rudy ignored Hathaway and went to say goodbye to Maria. As expected, he found her sleeping. Nurse Johansson was still sitting in the chair next to her. She told Rudy she would make sure she knew he had come by to say goodbye. Rudy nodded, unsure if that was a good idea. Maria might be disappointed that she missed him. Would she? he wondered. Yes, she would, he assured himself. Still, Rudy would have preferred to say goodbye. He found it upsetting that despite being stable, Maria looked worse than usual, spending far too much time sleeping. Rudy was well aware of her condition and her prognosis, but against his best instincts, he hoped.

"In certain instances, hope is a very dangerous thing," a surgeon had once told him.

He had resented the comment, but now he understood. He wasn't discouraging hope, not altogether, but reality came first.

Rudy returned to the nurses' station and got busy with the notes. It was late afternoon. He was free to go, but he didn't feel like leaving, and he certainly didn't feel like studying. Mike was on call, and he had been spending some of his free time with Julia, but they didn't have any plans. So Rudy didn't know what to do.

He ended up getting some notes done. That would help Andropov; maybe he could get home to his family early. Did he have a family, a wife, a girlfriend? Rudy realized he had no clue.

Suddenly, something was dropped on the counter in front of him. Looking up, he saw a medium-sized cardboard box decorated in a Christmas motif. It was covered with bright red wrapping paper. Embossed on it were several snowmen and red-nosed Rudolphs. In a word, it was cheesy. Behind the box, Nurse Hathaway was staring at him.

"What are you still doing here?" Hathaway asked.

"Not in a hurry to leave. Andropov could use the help."

"What about your girlfriend?"

"I don't have a girlfriend," replied Rudy, exasperated.

"What about that girl you are seeing, the model?" Hathaway asked.

Rudy swore he surely blushed. How could she know about Julia? But he instantly answered his own question: Mike.

"She's not my girlfriend, she's just a friend," Rudy replied shyly.

"That's not what your friend Davenport tells us."

Rudy fumed silently but smiled.

"We are just friends."

"I see."

Rudy looked once more at the box, his curiosity getting the better of him. He stood up and tried peeking inside the box.

"Christmas wishes, letters for Santa," Hathaway explained.

"From the children?" Rudy inquired.

Hathaway nodded.

"How do you get the gifts?" Rudy asked.

"We have donations . . . some of the parents, those that can chip in, we all do. Doctor Betances does a lot himself," Hathaway replied.

"What if they ask for something really expensive?" Rudy asked.

Hathaway smiled. She moved behind the counter and sat next to Rudy. There she began sorting the envelopes inside the box. After she had them all in a neat stack, she handed a few to Rudy.

"Why don't you read some of these? Just do one at a time and place it back in its envelope, so we know who it is from," Hathaway said.

Rudy didn't feel right about prying into their Christmas wishes, and Hathaway seemed to notice.

"Go ahead, it will answer your question."

Rudy decided to do as she asked, but he made sure not to look at the names, trying to respect the children's privacy. He picked the first envelope, reached inside it, and pulled out a folded paper. Carefully unfolding it, he began to read.

> *Dear Santa:*
> *All I want for Christmas is for my dad and mom to be with me all day. Please make it so dad doesn't have to work that day.*
> *Thank You.*

Rudy quickly folded the paper back, but he had seen the boy's name and felt a giant weight on his chest. He placed the paper back in the envelope and handed it back to Hathaway. She in turn handed him a few more letters.

"No, I get it," Rudy said.

"Read some more," Hathaway insisted.

Rudy continued, handing back each letter as he finished reading it. Every single one was a different request. Some did ask for gifts, but they were minor things. But without fail, even the children that asked for gifts always seemed to ask for something more. One asked for Santa to make sure his sister never became as sick as him. Another, a very sick girl, asked Santa to help the girl in the room next to hers get better. All asked to be able to spend more time with their family. They told Santa how much they wished to go back to the beach, or camping with their parents. Many asked for ice cream, which made Rudy smile involuntarily. The last one struck Rudy hard, and he continued to see the words long after reading them.

Please, Santa, make Mommy smile like she did before I was sick.

His throat felt tight, his breathing labored, and his eyes burned. Rudy turned and met Hathaway's gaze.

"Children know what's really important. They know what really matters, much more than we do. When their time is short, they want the only thing that has value," Hathaway said.

Taking a deep breath, Rudy rubbed his eyes with his right hand. They burned, and he felt the tears that had silently welled up. Reluctantly he took the letters, slowly going over the names written on them. When he finished, he realized there wasn't a letter from Maria. Rudy gazed back at Hathaway, for a second unsure if he should inquire.

"There's no letter from Maria," Rudy finally managed.

"There was, but someone is already taking care of her wish," Hathaway said.

Rudy hesitated, but curiosity won out.

"What did she ask for?" Rudy asked.

"She asked for what she most desires," Hathaway said, her voice broken. "You better go home and get some rest."

Knowing she would tell him no more, Rudy reluctantly left.

CHAPTER 22

On his way home, Rudy drove past a small upscale mall, which he knew had a large bookseller. This made him recall the book he was reading with Maria. On a whim, Rudy made an illegal U-turn, heading back to the mall. He drove into the parking lot, intent on getting his own copy.

He had trouble finding a parking spot near the main entrance, which Rudy found odd given the late hour. As soon as he was inside the mall, he realized the mall was full of Christmas shoppers. Rudy was oblivious to the season, and he nodded knowingly. During their medical training, students, residents, and fellows are so consumed by their studies and training that they become isolated from the world around them. After watching many of his attendings, Rudy sometimes wondered if that changed after training. Before, he had not really cared if that meant he would have been ranked as top dog. Now he wasn't so sure that he wanted this.

As Rudy walked to the store, he noticed a coffee shop that he had seen often enough, but never like tonight. It was so crowded that it looked more like a bar than a coffee place. Directly across from it was the bookstore. Rudy had a clear mission. He had no time to browse, so he quickly asked one of the store's employees for a copy of *The Little Prince*.

"I'm sorry, sir. We are all out," replied the employee.

"Really?" asked Rudy.

"Two high schools assigned it for Christmas reading."

Surprised to learn that they didn't have any copies of the book, Rudy thanked the employee and turned to leave.

"If you want, I could order it for you. I'll call tomorrow, and it may get here before New Year's. Your kid would have just a couple of days to read it, but that's better than nothing."

Rudy nodded. He had to admit it was weird for a twenty-something guy to be asking for what he considered a children's book.

"That's okay, serves him right," Rudy replied, thinking it was best not to clarify.

The employee shrugged and went about his business.

Rudy was sure he would find the book somewhere else, deciding that not finding it was a sign that he should head home and get some studying done. He was about to leave when he decided to get some coffee before heading home, as the place didn't look as full as before.

Rudy walked into the coffee shop to find it was still brimming with people talking loudly and sitting around tables. Again he thought it looked more like a bar at happy hour than a coffee shop. Regardless, Rudy got in line, glancing around until he saw a bunch of newspapers on a table beside the line. Thinking that the long line might actually allow him to get some updates on current events, he reached for one of the papers. To his surprise, someone jerked the paper away. Rudy looked, glaring, only to find Julia smiling back at him.

"What are you doing here?" Julia asked before hugging him tightly.

"Coffee," Rudy pointed to the far counter.

"There are a hundred coffee places near your place. Are you stalking me?" Julia asked, still smiling.

"How would I know you were here?" Rudy asked in turn.

Julia shrugged, clearly faking disbelief.

"Okay, I'm stalking you," Rudy answered, throwing his arms up.

"Should I call the police, or could we work this out ourselves?" Julia asked, frowning unconvincingly.

"What did you have in mind?" Rudy asked.

"Tacos and margaritas at Venice Beach," Julia said.

"Why not," Rudy replied, moving out of the coffee line.

"Really? That easy?" Julia asked.

Rudy understood her disbelief; his usual self would have required a lot of convincing. A couple of weeks ago he would have preferred to go home and get some studying done, but not today. Since she seemed to genuinely enjoy spending time with him, he actually welcomed the distraction, and he had fun with Julia. For a second, he smiled silently. The irony was that when Rudy first met Julia, he had been extremely intimidated. After all, she was a famous model. But as he had gotten to know her, he had come to learn she was fun and down-to-earth. He smiled again before speaking.

"Yeah. But I'm on call tomorrow, so I can't be out all night," Rudy said.

"I'll have you home by ten. I have an early day. I'm leaving for Hawaii early. Work," Julia said.

"How long?" Rudy asked.

"Four days," Julia replied.

"Why don't you tell me all about it during dinner?" Rudy said.

"Sure," Julia said. "Let me get my purse."

Reaching for Rudy's hand, Julia pulled him along. In fact, it was more like she dragged him around the place until they came to a table filled with what he could only guess were friends of hers from work, since they all looked like models or TV stars.

"Girls, I'm leaving you, I got myself a man," Julia said, reaching for her bag.

"Does this man have a name?" asked one of them as she eyed Rudy.

"Everyone, this is my friend Rudy," Julia said.

"Hi, Rudy," all of them replied in chorus.

The one closest to Rudy turned and with a sly smile looked Rudy over.

"So this is Rudy," she said. "Aren't you a little young to be a doctor?"

"Ignore Val," Julia told Rudy.

"It's fine. I'm not a doctor yet. I'm graduating from school in the spring," Rudy replied.

"Very nice," Val replied.

"Okay, okay. Say good night, girls," Julia said.

"Good night, Doctor Rudy," they all said, laughing.

Julia reached for Rudy again and dragged him away.

"I'm sorry about that. They aren't that bad. You know what's funny? Tomorrow they'll be begging me to fix them up with some of your friends," Julia said.

"Them? But aren't they models too?" Rudy asked.

"Yes, and we attract a lot of sleaze. Nice men are intimidated by us, just like you were," Julia said.

"I wasn't!" Rudy protested, shaking his head.

Julia smiled and kissed Rudy on the cheek.

"Promise me that you'll never play poker," Julia said.

Rudy laughed.

CHAPTER 23

It was early in the morning and the roads were still far from full. Feeling rested for the first time in more than a week, Rudy drove to the hospital, surprised he was making great time. He even managed to arrive at the hospital earlier than Andropov and Betances.

Now on the ward, Rudy walked down the hallway and behind the nurses' station as he searched for Mike. Rudy went into the on-call room, thinking Mike was probably sleeping, but the room was empty. And just like the last time Mike had been on call, he was nowhere to be found. Rudy suspected Mike might be having a fling with someone in the hospital. Although it seemed out of character for Mike, his disappearances almost confirmed it, at least in Rudy's mind.

With mild indifference, Rudy went on to get everything ready for the day's work. He set up the charts on the cart and printed out all the recent labs. Rudy was almost done when Mike appeared out of nowhere.

"You are early," Mike said.

"Morning. Where were you?" Rudy asked.

"Checking on Megan. She went into respiratory distress last night. We had to intubate her," Mike said.

"Damn," Rudy said.

"A post-intubation chest X-ray is negative. We did bronchial lavage for culture and gram stain," Mike said, catching his breath before he continued. "Her blood cultures came back positive for pseudomonas."

"Did you adjust antibiotic therapy?" asked Andropov, who was walking up to the far side of the nurses' counter.

"Yes, I called the infectious disease fellow to confirm," Mike replied.

"Good," Andropov replied.

"Anything else we should know, Doctor Davenport?" asked Betances.

Rudy hadn't noticed his arrival until he spoke. However, he was clearly aware of the situation. Mike fumbled inside his left pocket, producing a folded paper. It was a patient list, and he started to read from it. Mike dutifully listed every patient in the ward, and a few of the consults he was supposed to follow during the night. For each patient, he gave a small review of the night's events, if any. The night had been unremarkable for most of the patients, except for Megan, who had turned for the worse a few hours before dawn.

"Maria had no change?" asked Betances as he looked over Megan's chest x-ray.

"Her vitals are stable, but they keep getting . . ." Mike hesitated.

"Getting what?" Betances asked.

"She's clearly weak, more so than before," Mike added.

"Her body is slowly shutting down, Doctor Davenport. What do you propose we do now?" Betances asked.

"Keep her comfortable," replied Mike.

"That's all we can do," Betances said as they headed to Megan's room.

Inside, Rudy saw Bruce sitting hunched over his daughter. His head was raised and he looked intently at his daughter, who now had a tube taped to her mouth, the machine next to her helping with her breathing. As soon as he heard the group come in, Bruce stood up, his eyes pleading with a look of desperation Rudy was sure he would never forget. Betances walked close to the man and spoke in a low, hushed tone. He explained that now that she had a more specific antibiotic treatment, and that they might see improvement in the next few days. Bruce's eyes were glazed over, a testament to last night's ordeal.

"I'll check on her during the day. Have the nurse call us if anything changes," Betances said.

"What if she doesn't get better?" Bruce asked.

Rudy, who had been checking on Megan's fluids, turned to look at Bruce as he heard the question. From the man's expression, Rudy knew he was well aware of what that would mean. And for Rudy, the mere suggestion of the possible answer, which he also knew, made him feel as if the air in the room had been sucked away. With a sense of foreboding, Rudy watched Betances place his hand on Bruce's shoulder, his expression hard as he spoke.

"We pray for her," Betances said.

With tears in his eyes, Bruce pulled Betances close and hugged him, allowing himself to cry. Rudy watched as Betances returned the gesture and felt the ground fall away from his feet. For what seemed an eternity, the room fell into silence. It was a moment later that Bruce released Betances and made a motion of straightening his shirt.

"I'm sorry," Bruce said.

"No need to be. We all have to be strong. We have to be strong for her," Betances said.

He sounded reassuring, but Rudy could swear that for a split moment, Betances allowed himself a glimpse of hopelessness.

"I promise I'll be back soon," Betances said, and motioned everyone to leave.

Betances left the room, silently followed by Andropov, Mike, and lastly Rudy, who was in a daze.

Once more, Rudy felt misgivings about his chosen profession. These situations happened far more often than he thought he could handle. Was he really cut out to be a doctor?

***

Sometime later, they went ahead with rounds, moving down the corridor in sequence. Unlike before, the group moved in a stupor, their usual academic discussions muted and short-lived, their well-coordinated swiftness lost. They were about to walk past the doors leading to the isolation room when Nurse Ramirez blocked their way.

"She just fell asleep. Johansson is with her," Ramirez said.

Betances nodded, turning and heading back to the nurses' station. Like ducklings following their mother, everyone followed Betances back down the hall. As they did, Rudy noticed Mike glance back and forth at Betances. Rudy realized Mike's face suggested puzzlement. And with each glance, Mike seemed to be calling Betances' attention. Abruptly, Betances came to a halt, glaring back at Mike.

"Spit it out," Betances said.

Rudy watched as Mike swallowed hard before speaking.

"Doctor, you told that man to pray, but you—" Mike managed before Betances interrupted him.

"Rumor has it that I have no particular beliefs," Betances said.

"Yes," Mike replied.

"It's true, but if it gives solace to these suffering parents, if they want me to, I'll pray to a golden calf. If it makes these children happy for one more day, I'll sell my soul to the devil. Clear?" Betances asked.

"Yes," Mike replied.

Betances glared at Mike again, then headed back down the long hallway, his white robe flowing behind him.

***

True to his word, Betances returned to check on Megan several times that day and stayed on well past his usual time, making sure the girl did not deteriorate further. So it was quite late when Rudy found himself alone in the ward. He had just done a quick round, checking once more on Megan. After writing down orders for labs to be drawn in the early morning, Rudy headed down to Maria's room. Earlier in the day he promised her to stop by as soon as he had some time, and to his surprise, he was actually looking forward to seeing the little girl.

"You're still awake!" Rudy remarked.

"Not tired," Maria replied in a drowsy voice.

Nurse Chen, who sat next to her, raised an incredulous eyebrow.

"Right. Mind if I keep you company for a while?" Rudy asked.

Maria nodded weakly. Chen got up and gave Rudy a silent nod, which he understood clearly. By now the nurses had acknowledged their unofficial roster and had included Rudy on it. Loneliness in a hospital was sad. Loneliness for a sick child was horrible. So even though they tried to make sure that Maria had someone with her most of the day, during the nights they made sure she was never alone. Rudy had learned that it was during the nights that patients felt the most forlorn and the most vulnerable. But Hathaway had confided in him that although Maria was a tough little girl, she was afraid of the dark.

"I see Bunny is with you," Rudy said.

Maria nodded as she held tightly to the toy.

"Want me to read to you?" Rudy asked.

"No," Maria replied, her voice weak.

"TV? There might be some cool infomercials right about now, probably an Australian guy doing something crazy," Rudy said.

Maria smiled but shook her head. "Tell me about you and your brother," she said.

"Sure," Rudy said, knowing she wanted to know about the jokes they played on each other. Rudy told the first story, laughing himself as he retold it. Maria giggled in delight.

It was late and Maria was having difficulty staying awake. Rudy had just finished one of his stories when Maria raised her gaze, looking intently at Rudy.

"Will you stay with me after I fall asleep?" Maria asked.

"Of course I'll stay with you," Rudy said.

"Thank you," replied Maria, turning to her side.

"You know, when I was your age, I was afraid of the dark, too. I believed there was a monster in my closet, but there really wasn't. Monsters aren't real; it's just our minds playing tricks," Rudy said, trying to reassure her.

Maria turned back, feigning a smile, which seemed to fight for footing with sadness.

"I know there's nothing inside the closet, but monsters are real," she said, and with a pained expression, she raised a trembling hand to touch her chest. Maria nodded as she gently tapped the area over her heart.

"Monsters are real. I have one inside me," Maria said in a tortured whimper before turning away.

Aghast, Rudy felt the air blown out of him. He knew, of course, the girl was right, and to say he was lost for words did not quite cover it.

Then, unexpectedly, Maria turned back to Rudy. It was clearly difficult for her, but she managed to face him. In the dimly lit room, Rudy had a hard time making out her features, but he could see she was serious.

"Are you my friend? I mean, really? Not just because it's your job?" Maria asked.

"I am," Rudy said.

"Can you keep a secret?" Maria asked.

"Yes," Rudy replied.

"You have to promise to keep my secret forever," Maria insisted.

Rudy nodded. "I do. I will."

"I know there's no monster inside the closet, and I'm not afraid of the dark. I just tell the nurses that so someone will stay with me during the night. You'll stay with me, won't you?" Maria asked.

Rudy nodded, now confused. Why did she want the company?

"You'll keep my secret?" Maria asked again.

Rudy nodded again.

Maria forced what must have been a difficult smile. A lone tear ran down her cheek. She again turned and lay down on her bed, moving so her back was to Rudy, who was now unable to see her face. Maria pulled her covers up and spoke in a low, broken voice.

"I don't want to be alone at night. All the children, all my friends who died . . ." Maria struggled to speak. "They all died at night. Children always die at night. I don't want to be alone at night. I don't want to be alone when I die."

CHAPTER 24

Rudy felt someone tugging at his shirt. Still half asleep, he heard a faint voice call him.

"Dell, Dell, wake up," Nurse Chen said.

Waking slowly, Rudy stood up. He had some difficulty, having taken quite some time to fall asleep. Now his back ached and his body was numb from sleeping in the uncomfortable chair. Dazed, Rudy checked his wristwatch; it was well past one in the morning.

"What's going on?" Rudy asked, rubbing the small of his back to massage the cramp out.

"Megan. You need to come to Megan's room. I'll stay with Maria," Chen said, her voice filled with urgency.

Rudy didn't hesitate, hurrying out of the room and quickly down the hall. Without thinking, he pushed the door into Megan's room open. Inside, he found a young female doctor working on Megan's ventilator. Bruce stood close by, a worried look on his face.

"Doc, I'm glad you're here," Bruce said, his tone begging. "Could you tell me what's happening?"

Rudy made a reassuring motion with his hands, wanting Bruce to know he planned to find out.

"You Dell?" asked the female doctor. "I'm Doctor Fergusson. Your patient was in respiratory acidosis."

"Was?" Rudy asked.

"Well, she's on her way out of it," Fergusson replied.

Rudy breathed a sigh of relief, turning to Bruce and nodding reassuringly.

"How did you know to come? Did one of the nurses call you?" Rudy asked doctor Fergusson.

"I'm the pneumo-critical care fellow, so every ventilator in the hospital gets automatically consulted to my service," replied Fergusson.

"I haven't seen you before," Rudy said.

"I like to check on ventilators after midnight. Less people and less doctors to get in my way," Fergusson said.

"Oh," replied Rudy, now confused as to why he was here. "So what do we do now?"

"Her acidosis was brought on by the ventilator settings for the most part. I will teach you how to avoid that," Fergusson said with a tone of authority. "Follow me, Dell. Mister Banner needs to get some rest."

She then picked up Megan's chart and what had to be her Filofax and walked out of the room.

Rudy watched her in surprise. At no time did she reassure Bruce, not one word. She had terrible bedside manner.

"Bruce, we'll be right outside," Rudy said before leaving.

Rudy spent the next few hours being taught and quizzed on everything that had to do with ventilators, acidosis, alkalosis, both metabolic and respiratory, as well as hypoxia and tachypnea. He learned a thousand more things, and was completely amazed that Fergusson did all that from memory, including all the calculations. It was past five in the morning when Fergusson left, but not before she checked on Megan. As before, she didn't say an encouraging word to Bruce, but she did address Rudy before leaving.

"She's compensated. Keep her like that," Fergusson said.

"Thank you," replied Rudy as he watched her leave.

"Is that good?" asked Bruce.

"Very good," Rudy said in a reassuring tone. "Get some rest. I'll be around."

"I'll try," Bruce replied.

Rudy walked out into the hall to find that Hathaway and the rest of the day nurses were already there.

"The girls told me Fergusson had you at it all night," Nurse Hathaway said.

"It was brutal," Nurse Kruspe said.

Shrugging in response, Rudy's head felt numb from all the information. Lack of rest played a part too, but he realized he was now better equipped to help Megan. Not only that, but Fergusson had given him a great review for his boards. It then struck him that thinking about the boards didn't make him anxious. In a way, it didn't mean as much as it had a few weeks back. Before, he had wanted to earn the best results so that he could be the best for the sake of school standings. Now that wasn't his driving force; now it was different. He didn't know why, but he didn't care.

"Here!" said Ramirez, handing Rudy a cup of her special coffee.

"Thanks, I think I need this," Rudy replied.

"How's Megan doing?" Ramirez asked.

"Surprisingly well. Her temperature has been down for the last few hours, the most recent cultures are negative, and her labs are great. Fergusson said that we may be able to get her off the ventilator in the next few days," Rudy said.

"That's good news," Ramirez said.

"Why don't you get some rest? An hour of sleep might do you good," Hathaway said. "We'll print out everything and have it on the charts before rounds."

Rudy checked the time on his wristwatch. If he hurried, he might get a little over an hour of sleep before everyone came in for the day.

"I'll do that, thank you," Rudy replied as he placed the now half-empty cup of coffee on the nurses' station counter and headed back to Maria's room.

"Johansson is with Maria. Go to the on-call room," Ramirez said.

"I promised Maria I would stay with her. I want to be there in case she wakes up," Rudy said.

Hathaway smiled, giving him a nod of approval.

Back in Maria's room, Rudy found Johansson sitting next to Maria. As expected, she was occupied with some paperwork. Rudy managed to see it was a medication inventory.

"I'll stay with her," Rudy said.

Without a word, Johansson stood up and left. Rudy sat in the reclining chair and not a second later was fast asleep.

Again, Rudy heard someone calling him. Groggily, he fought to open his eyes, but only managed to open one. Standing next to him was Nurse Hathaway.

"It's time," Hathaway said.

"Right," Rudy said.

"Good morning," Maria said.

"What are you doing awake so early?" Rudy asked.

Maria shrugged.

"Reading," she said.

"Dell," Hathaway said.

"Yeah," Rudy headed to the door. "I'll see you later," he told Maria.

"Okay," replied Maria.

It struck Rudy that Maria didn't look well. Her complexion was more ashen than he remembered, and her hands shook slightly as she held the book up. Maria seemed to notice that he was looking at her and smiled. Rudy returned the gesture. Inside him, a deep aching made him wonder if her time was coming near. He took a last look at her, hoping this was not the last time he saw her.

Just as Rudy walked out the door, Nurse Johansson passed him, silently moving into Maria's room. He turned and watched as Johansson sat next to Maria.

Back at the nurses' station, Rudy saw Betances and Mike. They had begun the day's work, silently acknowledging Rudy's arrival. It was obvious that he was late, but Betances said nothing. Andropov arrived several minutes later with a considerable bundle of folded papers.

"Seventeen consults," Andropov announced.

It was unusual, at least since Rudy had been there, for them to have such a large number of consults. These would be addressed once the ward's patients were all taken care of. Thus Rudy was very aware they were about to have a very long day.

***

It was almost six o'clock when they finally managed all the consults and returned to the oncology ward. They still had to do afternoon rounds. The long day was feeling heavy on Rudy's shoulders, especially after his mostly sleepless night.

"Dell, call your friend from pneumo. Have her come down. I want to see if we can start to wean Megan off that ventilator," Betances said.

"She's not my friend," Rudy said.

An internal voice told him not to clarify, but he did anyway. Betances glared at him, confirming it was unwise and needless.

"I'll go page her," Rudy said.

"Get her down here," Betances said in a demanding tone.

As instructed, Rudy walked back to the nurses' station and paged Doctor Fergusson. He sat down at the counter while he waited for her to call back. Dozing off several times, Rudy fought to stay awake, although the constant beeps and occasional alarms of the monitors helped. Ten minutes later, the phone rang. Rudy heard it, but in his stupor was late to reach for it, and Ramirez answered the call.

"It's for you," Ramirez said.

Rudy reached for the phone, fumbling with the receiver before he got a hold of it.

"Hello," Rudy said.

"Who is this?" Fergusson asked. She sounded displeased.

"This is Doctor"—Rudy cringed—"Dell. We met last night in the oncology ward."

"What do you want?" Fergusson asked.

"I'm calling to see if you could come down to the ward to check on Megan, Megan Banner," Rudy said.

"I'm busy. I'll get to her tonight," Fergusson replied, clearly annoyed.

Fearing she might hang up, Rudy spoke quickly. "Wait! Wait! It's Doctor Betances. He wants to discuss the possibility of weaning her off the ventilator," Rudy said.

"Is Betances there?" Fergusson asked, her tone different.

"Yes, he is waiting for you," Rudy replied.

"I'll be there in twenty minutes," Fergusson replied before hanging up.

"Next time lead with that," Ramirez said.

"What?" Rudy asked.

"No one will refuse anything asked by Betances, not in this hospital. He's the best; he could be making millions in private practice. Yet he stays here in an academic setting. Everyone knows that, so no one refuses his requests, nor dares to," Ramirez said.

Rudy shrugged.

"Coffee?" Ramirez asked.

Rudy nodded silently.

It was quite a bit longer than twenty minutes before Fergusson finally showed up.

"Where's Betances?" Fergusson asked.

"I'll go get him," replied Rudy.

Rudy ran down the corridor and found him inside Maria's room.

"Doctor Betances, Fergusson is here," Rudy announced.

Betances turned and glared at Rudy for a moment, then he returned to Andropov and Mike.

"Raise the oxygen. Maria, I need to take care of something. I'll be back in a while," Betances said before he left the room.

Everyone followed except Rudy, who stayed behind. He tried not to, but he couldn't help it; he stared at Maria. She looked worse, a lot worse. Her ashen complexion had turned pallid, and her skin looked washed out, almost like a ghost. Her once-expressive smiling eyes had lost their luster and seemed to have sunken. Her smile—her constant smile, which despite it all still remained—was but a shadow of its usual self, the sides of her mouth sagging.

"Is everything okay, Doctor Dell?" asked Johansson.

"Yes. I just wanted to say good night to Maria," Rudy replied.

"Good night," Maria said, but her voice was low and somber.

"I'll see you tomorrow, okay?" Rudy said.

Maria nodded. As she looked at him, Rudy felt a profound sadness. He knew what was coming.

***

Rudy ran with absentminded steps, reaching his colleagues beside the nurses' counter. There he found Betances in a heated discussion with Fergusson. He wanted to start weaning Megan off the ventilator, but she wanted to wait twenty-four hours. Rudy joined the group and this time was wise enough to remain silent.

"With all due respect, Doctor Betances, she was in respiratory acidosis less than twenty-four hours ago. She is doing very well, but we have to be cautious. We can start weaning her off tomorrow," Fergusson said.

"So tomorrow morning?" Betances said.

"Yes," Fergusson replied.

"Excellent. I'll expect you here bright and early," Betances said.

Rudy smiled. Fergusson had just fallen into a bear trap. If what Ramirez had told Rudy about no one refusing Betances was true, and from what he had seen it was, Fergusson had no choice.

"I'll be here before six a.m. My morning meeting starts at a quarter to eight. I have to leave before then," Fergusson said.

"I'm on call tonight. I'll be here," Andropov said.

"No, I need Dell. I taught him everything he needs to know to follow the ventilator. I don't have time to explain everything to you," Fergusson said.

"Don't patronize me. I'm board certified in pediatrics, and an oncology fellow!" Andropov protested.

"I'll be here," Rudy replied.

Andropov turned and glared at Rudy, who returned the glare and gestured, hoping Andropov caught on.

"Very well," Fergusson said before storming out.

"Doctor Andropov, you are in charge. I just agreed with her so that—" Rudy managed to say before Andropov cut him off.

"Yeah, I got it," replied Andropov in a more relaxed tone.

There was a fleeting silence, which was suddenly broken by Mike.

"Damn, your new girlfriend is not a happy camper. Julia is going to be jealous," Mike remarked.

"What?" Rudy said, turning to Mike. He found him grinning, as were Andropov and Betances, much to Rudy's surprise.

"Dell, go home. You are about to fall over. I need you here bright and early," Betances said.

"Get some rest, buddy," Mike said.

"I will," Rudy said.

Rudy left the ward with a deep sense of foreboding. His steps felt unsure, and his mind unwilling to consider what might come to be. He felt an urge to drive the idea from his mind, but it was there—ever present, inevitable. Slowly he continued, hoping that his fear did not become reality, and driven by the hope that he hadn't said goodbye to Maria for the last time.

CHAPTER 25

Arriving earlier than expected the next morning, Rudy found Andropov standing against the nurses' counter looking weary and disheveled. As Rudy recalled from yesterday, Andropov had been wearing his own scrubs, but now he wore a different set, hospital-issued and scruffy. Acknowledging Rudy as he moved closer, Andropov's face said it all. Something happened last night. Rudy's first thoughts were of Maria, then Megan. As if sensing Rudy's dread, Andropov shook his head, as if trying to appease him.

"We had a late-night admission," Andropov replied, his voice thick with emotion. "He didn't make it."

"Jeez, I'm sorry," he stopped, noticing Andropov looked ill. Instead Rudy asked, "Are you okay?"

Andropov nodded silently.

"Fergusson isn't here yet. Megan is doing very well though," Andropov said.

Rudy considered what to do next, turning to Andropov with an idea.

"Let's begin rounds early, at least until Fergusson shows up. Maybe you can head home early," Rudy said as he began loading the charts on the cart.

Unexpectedly, Betances walked into the ward. It was earlier than Rudy had ever seen him there. Close behind him Nurse Lopez carrying a bundle of clothes in her hands. Betances motioned the nurse closer, taking the bundle from her.

"Shower, change, and go get some sleep," Betances told Andropov as he handed him the bundle.

"Doctor, I—" Andropov began.

"You are no good to anyone in your state. Be back in four hours," Betances ordered.

Andropov and Rudy were exchanging confused glances when Betances growled, "Now!"

With his head hanging low, Andropov reached for the clothes. He then headed down the corridor and to the left where the small on-call room was. Turning, he glanced back once more at Rudy and Betances before entering the room.

Again thinking Andropov looked trampled, Rudy noticed Betances. It was then that he saw that the man's clothes looked worn, which was very uncharacteristic for him. And he definitely wore far more than a five o'clock shadow. Rudy suspected that Betances hadn't gotten any sleep either.

"Doctor, are you okay?" Rudy asked.

"No."

The candid answer surprised Rudy. This was the first time Betances had allowed Rudy to see that things actually got to him. It was just a glimpse, but it confirmed he was human after all. Betances reached for the cart, moving his hand over the charts until he found the one he was looking for.

"Come on. I want to check on Megan before your girlfriend gets here," Betances said.

The remark irked Rudy, but he just drew a deep sigh and followed Betances inside Megan's room. Bruce was still sleeping, thus they made an effort to make as little noise as possible. This effort became futile when Fergusson announced her entrance by loudly pushing the door open, violently waking Bruce in the process.

"Let's get this over with," Fergusson said, startled when she saw Betances. "Doctor Betances, I'm sorry. I didn't know you would be here."

"Please come with me outside," Betances said, motioning her to the door.

Fergusson walked out of the room, followed by Betances. Rudy moved to follow but Betances blocked his way.

"Please check on Megan. We won't be but a minute," Betances said.

Rudy nodded. He apologized to Bruce and went on to examine Megan. Megan's temperature was normal, her lungs were clean with good breath sounds, and she looked well, aside from the ventilator. Rudy then checked her labs. Follow-up cultures were negative and the rest of her labs were close to nominal. Rudy then sat with Bruce and discussed their plan to begin slowly weaning her off the ventilator.

Fergusson came back in. Her face was crimson, and her eyebrows were furrowed in what looked like a mixture of anger and frustration. Betances followed close behind.

"Dell, Doctor Fergusson is going to explain how to proceed with Megan. Come and find me when you are done," Betances said.

After he left, Rudy walked up to Fergusson, who stood next to the ventilator scanning all its readouts.

"How can I help?" asked Rudy.

Fergusson turned, her expression now one of rage, her eyebrows angled inward. She glared at Rudy for a moment, but then her demeanor softened.

"It's not your fault," Fergusson said.

"So what's the plan?" Rudy asked, deciding to ignore her disposition.

Fergusson went on to explain how they would change the ventilator settings slowly throughout the day. The plan was to first keep Megan breathing with help from the machine, slowly giving her the capability to take over, with the ventilator assisting when needed. If things went well, Fergusson was sure she could be free from the ventilator in a day. Rudy was not on call, but he would keep checking on Megan during the day and adjusting the ventilator further until three o'clock as planned.

"I'll wait a couple of hours to make sure she's fine before I leave," Rudy said.

"This is my personal pager number. Page me if you need any help. I'll check on her tonight, and I'll be by tomorrow morning, same time as today," Fergusson said.

"I'll be here. Thank you," Rudy said.

A few minutes later, Rudy joined Betances and Mike, who seemed to have arrived while Rudy was in Megan's room. They went on with rounds, which were mostly unremarkable, finishing at Maria's room. She was still asleep, which was becoming the norm for her. Her vitals were stable, but everything was slowing down. Although she was not bradycardic, her pulse was unusually slow for a girl her age. Checking her chart, Rudy could see that she had a rough night.

"Her body is just too weak, but her spirit is so very strong. That's why she's still here; that's why she fights," Betances said before becoming silent.

Rudy recalled Betances had said this before, and he began to wonder if he said it more for his benefit than for hers. Mike and Rudy exchanged looks before Rudy gazed at the sleeping Maria, understanding what Betances's silence meant. His implication was clear. She had survived thus far, but the moment was soon coming when she would survive no further.

"Stay with her," Betances said.

Rudy moved to sit next to the bed, reaching for a few charts from the cart.

"Just stay with her. I'll deal with those," Betances said as he reached for the charts in Rudy's hands.

Once alone, Rudy crouched forward in the recliner next to Maria's bed, disquieting thoughts taking over. He moved in the chair but failed to find a more comfortable position. He sat back. Rudy had the nagging suspicion his discomfort had nothing to do with the chair. Suddenly he felt something between the cushions. Reaching between these, Rudy found a folded book. It was the board review book he had been studying. For a while he flipped through the pages, reading here and there, doing so mostly to pass the time, as his mind was distracted, distant. About an hour later, Maria woke. She turned, scanning the room and smiling widely, although with clear surprise, when she saw Rudy.

"How long did I sleep?" Maria asked.

"Not really sure," Rudy said, realizing she had been expecting to find one of the nurses.

"Oh," she said as she rubbed her eyes with the back of her hands.

"How do you feel?" Rudy asked.

She shook her head slowly and shrugged in a very childlike way. Rudy knew what she meant.

"Want anything to eat?" Rudy asked, knowing how she would answer.

"No," she replied as expected.

"Something on the TV?" Rudy asked.

"No, what are you reading?" she asked, her voice groggy. To Rudy's dismay, he could tell it was not from drowsiness.

"Behavioral science, for the test I told you about," Rudy replied.

"What's that?"

"Psychiatry," Rudy said.

She frowned for an instant, as if trying to figure out the word. Then a smile of understanding flashed across her face.

"Crazy people doctors," Maria said.

"Yes, you could say that. A bit politically incorrect, but it's certainly driving me crazy," Rudy said with a snicker.

"Read me something?" Maria asked.

"From this?" Rudy asked surprised.

"Um-hum," she replied.

"No, no, no. It's terrible. It will put you to sleep," Rudy replied.

"I'm tired. Please," Maria said.

Coming to grips with the situation, Rudy took a deep breath. He swallowed hard and did his best to maintain some evenness in the tone of his voice, something which was becoming increasingly difficult. Rudy had been reviewing personality disorders, which he wasn't about to read to Maria. Flipping back and forth, he came to basic science. Rudy silently nodded and started reading aloud; not loudly, just loud enough for Maria to hear him. Rudy continued to read for some time, feeling drowsy himself. It didn't take long before Rudy closed the review book and turned to Maria, who was fast asleep.

Rudy carefully pulled the covers up and moved her bunny close to her. He then made sure the oxygen mask still did its job, but was not too tight. Rudy sat back and again reached for the review book, flipping back to personality disorders, but found it impossible to read.

It was a little more than an hour later when the door to the room opened slowly. Rudy turned to find Nurse Hathaway, followed by a young boy and a woman. They had been dutifully outfitted in the protective gowns, which was the norm when entering the room. They moved in slowly, as if uncertain. They were followed close behind by Betances.

With numb legs, Rudy slowly raised from the chair, surprised by Betances, who was wearing something Rudy had never seen him wear—a real smile.

"This is Billy," Betances said.

Rudy was confused for a split second, but then it registered. "Billy! Maria's Billy," Rudy said. "But how?"

"He's here, that's all that matters." Betances said waving Rudy's questions away.

Betances knelt beside the boy, who seemed reluctant to move close to the bed.

"Go on. It's okay," Betances encouraged him.

"I won't make her sick?" Billy asked.

Betances shook his head. "No. On the contrary, you'll make her very happy," Betances added.

Billy moved closer. He hesitated, moving carefully as he came as close as he dared to the sleeping girl. When he saw her face hidden behind the oxygen mask, Billy smiled a true, heart-warming smile. But it faded when he saw the ravages of the illness on Maria's face. His smile weakened and his expression, which had been one of joy, now fought for equal billing with what must have been utter sadness. Billy placed his hand on Maria's shoulder, and lovingly and with great care, he shook Maria in an attempt to wake her. After a few tries, Maria slowly opened her eyes. Billy crouched, coming to eye level with Maria, who frowned as she woke up and clearly struggled to take in what was happening. Maria took a moment, gazing at the face of her most unexpected visitor. Confused, but just for a moment, she jumped up as best as she could and hugged the boy. Maria didn't speak. She just pulled the boy close to her, holding on tightly. Billy returned the gesture as the two of them cried and laughed loudly.

"I think they could use some time for themselves," announced Betances, motioning everyone to the door.

Mike and Rudy nodded in unison, retreating. Betances smiled as he gazed at the children. He was turning to leave when Maria called him.

"Thank you," Maria said, her voice shallow, broken but full of gratitude.

"You are most welcome."

Silently, Rudy followed Betances and Mike out of the room and past the isolation doors. Moving back to the nurses' station, Rudy's mind raced. How had Betances managed to find Billy? Rudy's friend Chuck had told him it would take some time, private investigators, and a lot of money, and even then it was a long shot.

"Davenport, stay here. Make sure Maria and her guest get everything they need. I'll take care of the consults," Betances said.

Rudy reached for Megan's chart when Betances addressed him. "How's Megan doing?"

"On schedule. I'm supposed to change settings in half an hour," Rudy replied.

"Keep at it. What if she doesn't respond to the changes?" Betances asked.

"I'll go back to full ventilation and page Fergusson."

"Page me and wake Andropov," Betances said.

Rudy nodded before succumbing to the urge to ask about Billy and how he managed to get him here.

"It's Christmas, Dell. It is the time of miracles," replied Betances, faking a German accent and smiling.

Rudy smiled. He didn't get the quote, but he had no intention of letting anyone in on his ignorance.

CHAPTER 26

The next morning, Rudy walked into the ward earlier than anyone expected. He was hoping to get a jump on Fergusson, which he managed. As expected, Mike was not at the nurses' station, or inside the on-call room. By now Rudy was quite sure his friend was having a fling somewhere in the hospital. Maybe it was more than just a fling. Rudy sure hoped it was. The idea that Mike had found someone from the real world appealed to Rudy. Rudy meant it in a good way. Someone who saw the world differently might be good for Mike.

For as long as Rudy could remember, Mike had been surrounded by beautiful women. But even to the most casual observer, it was clear that they were with Mike because of who he was. It was also painfully clear to Mike, who always kept them at arm's length for the most part.

When Rudy first met Julia, he had misjudged her, thinking she was one of those. Surprised that Mike allowed her close, Rudy quickly realized she was different, and a true friend to Mike.

If Mike had found someone, if this was the case, Rudy was glad for Mike. Still, he should have been back by now.

Getting on with his work, Rudy printed all the patients' most recent lab work. He then reached for Megan's chart, checking to see how she had done during the night. Rudy was relieved to see that everything checked out. He was about to go check on Megan when he saw Chen at the far end of the nurses' counter. Walking up to her, he decided to inquire about Mike.

"Where is Davenport?"

"Checking on some of the patients. You are here early," remarked Chen.

"I'm supposed to meet Doctor Fergusson."

"Really? That cute little pneumo fellow?"

"It's not like that. She's helping with Megan's ventilator."

"Sure she is."

Rudy glared at Chen, but before he could say anything, Hathaway, who seemed to have arrived a few seconds before, joined the conversation.

"Chen, leave the boy alone. That Doctor Fergusson might be very good at what she does, but I just don't like her," Hathaway said.

"Why?" asked Rudy.

"She's conceited, and—" Hathaway cut herself short.

"And?" Chen asked.

"Yes, and?" Rudy asked.

"I think she grew up as a little princess and still thinks she's one," Hathaway said with a sigh.

"Who's a princess?" came a voice from behind them.

Turning, Rudy found himself face to face with Fergusson. Surprised and in a panic, Rudy's mind flew all over the place trying to find a way to explain the comment away.

"Johansson, Nurse Johansson," replied Chen in a reassuring tone.

Fergusson nodded, turning to Rudy.

"Here, I brought you some coffee," Fergusson said.

"Thanks," replied Rudy as he took a sip of what had to be the most dreadful coffee he had ever tasted.

"Do you have her chart?" Fergusson asked.

"Megan's?" Rudy asked.

Fergusson reached into her pocket for a small notebook. She flipped it open and thumbed the pages until she came to what she was looking for.

"Banner, Megan, yes," Fergusson said.

"All her lab work is already inside," Rudy said as he handed her the chart.

"Good. Is there anywhere we can sit and go over this before we go see her?" Fergusson asked.

"Follow me," Rudy said.

Rudy motioned her to the lounge beside the nurses' counter. Chen grinned at Rudy mockingly. Unable to say anything, Rudy rolled his eyes. In a moment, Fergusson and Rudy moved to the small lounge area hidden at the side of the nurses' station. There they sat and discussed Megan's progress, her labs, and the last ventilator settings.

"This is more than we discussed," Fergusson remarked.

"Yeah, I managed to get her on the assist earlier than expected," Rudy said proudly.

"That was reckless, and not what we discussed," Fergusson said.

"I'm sorry, I—" Rudy began.

"It worked, but from now on we follow my plan," Fergusson said.

"Yes," Rudy replied.

"I'm on call today, so I'll be around. You?" Fergusson asked.

"I am," Rudy replied.

"Excellent," Fergusson said enthusiastically.

"Let's get moving. We'll dial down the assist further and follow her. I'll write down the settings and the instructions. Small adjustments during the day," Fergusson said.

"I will, and I'll keep checking on her every few hours," Rudy said.

"If this works, I'll have her off the ventilator by tomorrow morning," Fergusson said.

***

Fergusson left about an hour later, allowing Rudy to join Andropov, Mike, and Betances at the nurses' station.

"Rounds over?" Rudy asked.

"Just about. We still have to see Megan and Maria," Andropov replied.

"How are we doing with Megan?" Betances asked.

"Very well. We just dialed the assist down. I'll do two more dial downs during the day. Fergusson thinks that if all goes well, she can have Megan off the ventilator tomorrow," Rudy replied.

"*You'll* have her off the ventilator. You are doing most of the work; take credit. Are you sure you want to be a plastic surgeon?" Betances asked. "You could be a real doctor."

But he did not wait for an answer, instead heading down the hall and out of the ward. He was almost at the door to the elevators when he turned.

"Go check on Maria. I need to get Billy up."

Andropov, Mike, and Rudy headed in the opposite direction to Maria's room. Once inside, Rudy saw something completely unexpected. The day before, Maria had been very weak. She had slept most of the day and refused to eat anything. She had been pallid, her face wasted, her eyes sad and sunken. Today she looked completely different. She still looked ill, but her color was back, and she even had a subtle shade of pink in her cheeks. Her eyes sparkled and seemed to smile as she smiled herself. Unlike yesterday, she was full of energy. She looked alive. Lastly, to Rudy's surprise she was eating, and with what seemed like great delight.

"Is that ice cream?" Mike asked.

Maria nodded as she chewed on a waffle. "And waffles."

Rudy couldn't help but smile. Her voice seemed so vivid, so foreign from the girl he had seen yesterday. He was delighted to see her like this.

"You look well. How do you feel?" asked Andropov.

"Good, hungry," Maria said between mouthfuls.

Rudy smiled, turning to Mike, who wore a big grin. He then turned to Andropov for confirmation. To Rudy's surprise, Andropov's face was hard. There was no question, Andropov looked worried. Rudy was about to ask him what was wrong when Betances came in with Billy in tow.

"Good morning," Betances said loudly.

"Billy!" Maria said with joy.

"What in God's name are you eating?" Betances asked.

"Waffles, walnuts, blueberries, and rocky road ice cream," Maria said.

"That's disgusting. I love it," Betances said.

Maria and Billy laughed loudly at the comment.

"I know what we are having for lunch, all of us," Betances added.

"I'm lactose intolerant," Andropov said.

Betances made a comical face, or his best attempt at one.

"You know what that means?" Betances said in a low voice.

Maria and Billy shook their heads, smiling in anticipation.

Betances hunched over to be closer to the children, cupping one hand over his mouth as if to keep a secret while he answered his own question in one word: "Farts."

Maria and Billy laughed and snorted in a display of true joy. Rudy could not help but admire Betances. It had always struck Rudy how Betances could manage such turnarounds, especially with the kids. How he knew how to work with them and make them feel like they were his equals. When he first got here, Rudy had believed Betances was disrespectful with the children. He now knew the children loved and appreciated his unconventional bedside manner.

"Billy, you want some of that?" Betances pointed to Maria's tray, waving his hand over it. "That stuff."

Billy shrugged.

"Andropov," Betances said.

"I'll tell Hathaway," Andropov turned to a phone in the corner.

"So what's the plan?" Betances asked Maria.

"We saw *Star Wars* yesterday. We are going to watch *Empire*," Maria said.

"First time?" Betances asked Billy.

Billy nodded silently.

"Dell, you like those, right?" Betances asked.

"Sure," Rudy said.

"Why don't you join them later? Well, if they don't mind. Maria?" Betances asked.

Maria nodded between mouthfuls.

"I'll send Dell back in a few minutes. People, follow me," Betances said.

The team walked out of the room and into the main hallway. While they gathered, Hathaway passed by them with the tray for Billy.

"Dell, it's better if you are here to keep working on Megan's ventilator. You can come in and out and watch the movie with them. Keep an eye on Maria. I don't like how she looks," Betances said.

"But she looks great. I haven't seen her this well, this alive, since I got here," Rudy said with puzzlement.

"That's what scares me," Betances said.

CHAPTER 27

It was late in the night, and as usual when all the work was done, Rudy had gone to keep Maria company. She had watched TV with Billy, so she wanted Rudy to read to her if he could. He read to her until she fell asleep. A few minutes later, Rudy fell asleep as well. It was past midnight when Rudy woke, startled. He turned to Maria, who was still sleeping. He then gazed up at the vital signs monitors and breathed a sigh of relief. Although he was exhausted, Rudy remembered he still needed to get some charts in order before he could call it a night. But since he had forgotten them at the nurses' station, he needed to go down and get them. Maria wouldn't wake up while he hurried to get the charts, and he was sure nothing would happen during the few minutes he would be away. Carefully opening the door, Rudy came out of isolation and found Nurse Chen just outside the doors on a medications round. When he explained, she offered to keep an eye on Maria while he got the charts.

Hurrying, Rudy reached the station and gathered the charts. As he did, he noticed several printouts loosely gathered on the counter. These turned out to be new lab and pathology reports. Rudy hadn't expected to find them but decided to sort them before going to sleep. So he placed them on top of the chart and was heading back to Maria's room when Nurse Chen came running down the hall.

"Maria's up. She's not well," Chen managed.

Dropping everything, Rudy ran to Maria's room. His breathing faltered as he ran down the hall, which now seemed to go on forever. With his heart pounding, Rudy pushed the doors open past the small corridor before Maria's door. He decided to forego the protective coverings, as Rudy was sure it was of no use anymore, and Maria deserved to be met without the paper barriers. Inside he found Nurses Smith and Bellaire, who were already working on Maria. One made sure Maria's oxygen mask was properly placed as she raised the oxygen rate. The other exchanged her half-empty saline bag for a full Ringer's lactate. Bellaire drew blood and ran outside, vial in hand.

Chen arrived a moment later, dragging the crash cart behind her. She quickly filled a syringe from a small glass vial. After exchanging the needle tip, she injected the medication into the tubing snaking down from the Ringer's and into Maria's central line.

"Hey, Maria. Feeling okay?" she asked.

"No," Maria shook her head slowly, her voice low and weak. "I feel funny, tired, sleepy but different."

Rudy smiled at Maria. She returned the gesture as best she could as her eyes fought to stay open and her body slumped back. It was as if the will to move had been drained out of it. Her face, which not a day before had beamed, now looked empty, pale, and vanquished.

Chen gazed up at the vital signs monitor. Rudy followed her gaze. Finding it, he could see Maria's vital signs. As he feared, her blood pressure was going down, along with her pulse. Rudy closed his eyes for a moment, overcome with a deep ache in the pit of his stomach, and his heart stung with each beat. Unconsciously, his body already knew what his mind was still trying to comprehend.

With difficulty, Maria turned her head, looking back at Rudy.

"I'm . . . I'm scared," Maria said in a painful whimper, her gaze a supplication.

Without hesitation, Rudy reached Maria, sitting next to her. He extended his arm so that Maria could move close to him, which she did, resting her head on Rudy's chest. Slowly she crossed her arms around her toy bunny. Then, as she embraced her toy, she moved her hands up close to her face. Closing them into half open fists, Maria placed one over the other and moved them up to her chin. She then allowed herself to fall on Rudy's chest. Moving with great care, Rudy gingerly placed his arms over Maria's frail body. It struck him that he couldn't really feel her; she felt so very insubstantial and frail. Maria stayed there, unmoving, eyes closed. For a moment, Rudy wanted to explain that he hadn't broken his promise, that he was not going to leave her to sleep alone, but there was no need to. Rudy was back with her and that was all that mattered.

A few minutes later, Doctor Andropov walked into the room, followed by Hathaway. Both looked shaken, their clothes witness that they had dressed in haste. Chen walked up to them and silently gave them a heads-up on the situation. Nodding silently, Andropov examined the monitors before moving close to Maria and Rudy. He gave Rudy a grim stare, his expression foreboding. After gently placing his hand on Rudy's shoulder, he leaned down to face Maria. He gently touched her back, placing his stethoscope next to Rudy's hand. After carefully moving the bell over a few points on Maria's back, Andropov got up and gave a few orders.

The nurses continued working, giving Maria medication after medication in the hopes her pulse and blood pressure improved, but they didn't. An out-of-breath Bellaire returned with a long printout, which she quickly handed to Andropov. After scanning the results, he moved closer to the crash cart and examined the notes made by the nurses.

"We are following protocol, Doctor," Chen replied.

Andropov nodded, but Rudy could see the change in his expression that gave him away. Despite all the treatment she was getting, Maria wasn't getting better. Rudy knew they were losing her.

It was then that the door opened loudly, and in a rush of motion, Mike entered the room. He wore a tux, which was in shambles, his tie loose and falling to one side as he moved. With haste, he removed his jacket, snapping off one his cufflinks, which flew to a corner, ricocheting repeatedly before coming to a stop.

When she saw him, Maria reached for him, and without hesitation Mike returned the gesture, picking the girl up. He embraced her and sat down in the large chair next to the bed. Maria's face lit up as much as her emaciated complexion allowed.

"I'm sorry, I'm sorry, I'm here," Mike said, his voice trembling.

Maria nodded slightly as she pressed her face into Mike's chest. Mike squeezed her slightly as he ran his hand over the scant stubble on her balding head. A few tears ran down her face, but she didn't make a sound, at least none that Rudy could hear. Rudy noticed that as she struggled to stay up, Mike moved so his hold was sure. This allowed Maria to relax and just rest. Mike grimaced with great sadness, not pain, but it was clear it was becoming overwhelming for him, as it was for everyone in the room. Silent tears ran down Mike's face. It was then that Rudy realized that he too was crying. Rudy felt an urge, and slowly turned his head, as if looking for something. Rudy immediately saw the fallen bunny beside the chair and rushed to pick it up. After reaching for it, Rudy knelt down beside Mike and Maria, looking at Mike for confirmation. He nodded, smiling painfully.

"Maria, here, honey," Rudy said, carefully moving the bunny so that she could embrace it. Mike released his grip ever so slightly so Maria could again embrace her beloved bunny. She did, but only managed to do so slowly. Mike again closed his arms around the girl. Still kneeling, Rudy frowned as a weak Maria struggled to open her eyes, lazily looking at the bunny now snuggled between her and Mike. She then raised her tired gaze to Rudy. With her eyes half open, she gave Rudy a slight nod. Forcing a thin smile, she mouthed a silent and clearly difficult thank you. Allowing her eyes to close, she pulled the bunny close, and Mike in turn pulled her closer and held her as tight as he could. Rudy could see Mike's tears. Maria made no sound, except for her breathing, which was becoming slower with every minute.

Rudy moved back, just a step, slowly coming to halt as he felt someone behind him. Rudy turned and saw Doctor Betances, who stood silently behind him, looking at Maria and Mike. Betances glanced at Rudy momentarily, allowing Rudy to see his somber expression. His eyes were bloodshot, his face flushed, as if angry, but all of them knew he wasn't. Rudy nodded and turned back, catching a glimpse of Mike's lips, which were moving. He was speaking what seemed to be a low, silent prayer, but Rudy was close enough and managed to catch the words. It was not a prayer, but it might as well have been.

"Maria, look there, see it? The great field, and just below the apple trees, you see them, don't you? So many rabbits, they are all waiting for you. They want you to chase them. Are you going to chase them?" Mike asked.

"Yes," Maria answered back in an imperceptible whisper.

"Yes, and you'll catch them, and they'll all be your friends," Mike continued, tears now flowing freely down his face.

Maria nodded with a faint smile.

"Look behind them. It's the brown bunny. He's waiting for you. He has been waiting for you all along. He's going to take you up to the moon," Mike said, his voice breaking.

Maria again nodded silently with a thin, faint smile.

Rudy felt out of breath as Nurse Hathaway walked closer and stood next to him. Rudy turned and saw her crying, her right hand covering her mouth. Rudy scanned the room. Even

Betances's hard, unemotional expression was betrayed as tears ran down his face. Mike raised his head. It was clear to everyone that he fought to keep his composure. Despite it all, Mike continued talking to Maria, describing the vast field, the running rabbits, and Maria's beloved bunny.

A few minutes later, when Maria, still in Mike's arms, deteriorated further, Andropov moved, addressing Chen in a hush tone.

"We need to intubate," Andropov said in a low voice.

"No. The next of kin signed a DNR," Doctor Betances announced.

Andropov glanced at everyone in the room, then back at Betances.

"Next of kin?" Andropov asked, surprised.

Betances nodded.

"This is what Maria wanted, and her family agreed. We have to respect that," Betances said.

"What family? She didn't have any family," Andropov said.

"She did," Betances replied.

"We were all her family," Hathaway said.

"We have to let her go," Betances placed his hand on Andropov's shoulder.

Andropov inhaled deeply as he looked at Maria and Mike, then turned to Rudy. In that moment, Rudy could see that Andropov had just acknowledged to himself that there was nothing they could do.

All the while, Mike kept telling Maria about the field and the running rabbits. Suddenly Maria opened her eyes and spoke, her voice low and weak, but Rudy managed to hear her, and he was sure everyone else did too.

"Don't be sad. I get to play with Bunny. I will wait for you, then we can play together," Maria said.

"Yes, I promise we will," Mike said as he allowed himself to cry silently.

Maria smiled, closing her eyes and reaching up for Mike. But her hand suddenly fell on his chest and her body sagged as she drew her last breath, the bunny falling to the floor.

CHAPTER 28

The room had fallen into a deafening silence that was broken only by the sustained electronic drone from the cardiac monitor. The sound was now a flat monotone. Rudy only noticed it was still on when Betances moved past everyone and turned it off.

Mike still held on to Maria, now more tightly as her arms no longer held on to him, her frail body unmoving. The toy bunny lay on the floor beside Mike. Mike's flushed face flashed a thousand emotions, all of them expressions of sorrow. Looking intently at Maria, Mike ignored everyone around him, his eyes fixed on Maria, his breathing slow and clearly labored. Quiet tears flowed down his face.

Rudy was sure he, too, showed the same mixed emotions Mike did. He, too, had felt it, and for the first time in his life Rudy felt truly lost. His heart stabbed at him and his body and soul were in agony. People talk all too easily about loss and having a broken heart. Rudy might have thought it in the past, but for the first time in his life, he really understood what it was to feel like you were going to die of a broken heart.

Unexpectedly, Mike got up. He carried Maria to the bed beside him and carefully placed her on it. Silently, he reached for gauze tape and other supplies and began freeing Maria from the monitors and IV lines on her body. He lovingly cleaned and bandaged the wounds afterward. Rudy watched him. He wanted to help, but thought better of it, seeing the love and respect Mike showed while he performed this most sacred ritual. He remained silent, as did everyone in the room. Once finished, Mike reached for the toy bunny on the floor and placed it next to Maria in such a way that her arm cradled the toy. Mike then moved back in utter silence. Mike caressed Maria's head as he gazed into her eyes, which he carefully closed. Standing back, Mike looked down at Maria, and for the longest of moments stood motionless beside her. Then, with a broken voice, he addressed the room.

"Thank you for being here. I'm sure Maria was thankful to have you all here."

With that, he moved closer to the bed and bent down, kissing Maria on her forehead before he turned and slowly left the room. As soon as Mike left, Betances spoke. It was then that Rudy noticed that Andropov was no longer inside the room.

"Andropov is making all the arrangements. Please help him," he told Nurse Chen. "Next of kin left instructions."

Next of kin. He had heard Betances say that before, but it was now, after all had passed, that it registered. Rudy was at a loss. She had no one. Billy was just a boy and not actually related.

"Doctor Betances, next of kin?" Rudy asked.

Forcing a smile, Betances nodded.

"Hathaway will explain," Betances said as he gazed down at Maria. He then touched the corner of the bed, frowned, and left the room.

Rudy turned to Hathaway, who sighed.

"Her next of kin," she said. "He's the one who found Billy and managed to bring him over. He's the one who gave Maria her bunny."

"I thought Betances did all that," Rudy said, surprised.

"No, he tried finding Billy, but he couldn't, and no one knew about the rabbits until after the toy bunny appeared," Hathaway said.

"Then who? And why didn't they show up before?" Rudy asked.

"She was adopted not two weeks ago, less than that. He came into her life not so long ago, and he did what he could in the short time he was here," Hathaway said.

Confused, Rudy tried to understand. It didn't make sense. Who adopted her? Rudy had been here for the last two weeks and he had seen no one. Then he had a thought. Rudy shook his head. It couldn't be, but who else? His eyes must have given him away. Hathaway nodded silently.

"Mike?" Rudy asked.

"Yes, he didn't want you to know," Hathaway said.

Rudy was overcome; he couldn't understand. Hathaway nodded again.

"With the exception of the nights you were on call, Davenport spent every moment he could here with Maria. He said that Maria enjoyed spending time with you, and he knew you were taking care of her, so he stayed away those nights when you were here. The rest of the time he was here, even when Andropov was on call. He made us keep it from you. It was Davenport who found Billy and flew him over here. We don't know how he did it, but he did," Hathaway said.

"How did he adopt her?" Rudy asked. "That takes time."

"Not when you have unlimited resources, and certainly not for someone like Davenport," Hathaway said.

"I need to talk to him," Rudy said.

Rudy moved out of the room and ran down the hallway to the nurses' station. He looked for Mike, but he wasn't there. Noticing Rudy, Nurse Chen shook her head.

"Davenport left."

Still unable to process what he had just heard about Mike, Rudy gazed at the long nurses' station. At the far end, he could see a patient chart with a sheet of paper on top of it. He guessed what it was—Maria's chart and her death certificate. Reluctantly, Rudy walked over to the far corner, when his attention was called to Megan's room.

"Dell," called Betances, motioning him inside Megan's room.

Unmindfully, Rudy walked to the room. Inside he found Doctor Fergusson beside Megan, who was no longer on the ventilator. She was just wearing a nasal cannula. She was breathing by herself and smiling broadly.

"Rudy," she said in a raspy voice, clearing her throat afterwards.

"Hey," replied Rudy, giving Megan a once-over. Her face was no longer pale. She was perky once more, and her eyes shone as they had the first day he met her.

"I feel better," Megan added.

"You look better," Rudy replied.

"If this keeps up, you'll soon be out of here." Betances said.

"Really?" Megan asked with excitement.

Betances nodded with a smirk.

"Can't get you out of here fast enough, kid," Betances said, feigning annoyance.

"Same here. I don't want to see your ugly face anymore," replied Megan.

"Megan!" Bruce said.

With another smirk, Betances extended his hand and offered Megan a high five, which she immediately returned.

"I'll see you later, kid," Betances said.

Betances, Fergusson, and Rudy met at the nurses' station outside, where they discussed Megan's case for a minute. Since Andropov was busy making all the necessary arrangements for Maria and Mike had disappeared, Betances asked Rudy to help him do rounds. Despite the early hour, most of the children were already awake and they could get an early head start.

"It will distract our minds," Betances said.

Rudy understood and moved silently from room to room behind Betances. Rudy suddenly found himself at the doors leading to isolation; for the first time since he arrived at the ward, Rudy would not be walking past them.

They returned to the nurses' station. Rudy continued down to the far end, picking up the chart that had been sitting in the corner. As he expected, it was Maria's, her death certificate fixed to the front cover. Rudy was about to read over it when an orderly asked him for the chart. Turning, Rudy could see the low gurney with Maria's small body covered by a white bed sheet.

"Doc, the chart," said the orderly.

Rudy looked down and managed to read one thing before handing the chart to the orderly: it was the next of kin's signature. He knew the penmanship well. It read *Mortimer Davenport.*

CHAPTER 29

Several days later, Rudy found himself at a private estate outside the city. He had been here before. It was a place he knew well—Mike's family home, if you could call it a home. By its size, it was more of a compound. It had expansive, trimmed, green fields filled with all sorts of trees and several lakes. The grounds were remarkable, with a great natural beauty. Today all of it was underscored by the dark gloom of the day. Far at the back, a large manor occupied a central spot near a neatly manicured garden. To the side, a few private roads led to several areas, including a private heliport. But that's not where Rudy was headed. He turned left and down the road to a private mausoleum nestled between some trees about a hundred yards from the main house. Still afar, but moving closer, Rudy could make out some of the faces. He recognized almost everyone. Rudy saw that most of the hospital staff was there, standing solemnly under the cold air, waiting.

Rudy parked and joined the group, nodding silently. Politely smiling in return, they nodded back, but no one spoke. As he made his way closer, some of the attendees moved in front of him, allowing him a clear view of the closed casket. Frowning, Rudy came to a halt, gazing at those who had moved aside. Their intent was clear. They didn't have to say anything. Rudy understood as he came to stand in plain view of the closed casket.

Sometime later, Mike came up the road. He carried Maria's toy bunny and walked flanked by Alfred. Coming closer to the group, Mike forced a smile as he faced the somber faces, but came to a halt when he got to Rudy. With a grimace, he reached for Rudy and hugged him tightly, allowing himself a painful, muffled sigh.

"Come, you were her family too," Mike said.

Rudy walked abreast with Mike and Alfred. None said a word, coming to stand in front of the casket. Rudy saw a tired, desolate look on Mike's face. He could only guess he, too, wore such a semblance. Mike's arms fell to his side. In his right hand, he still held Maria's prized plush Bunny. Alfred stood to Mike's left and Rudy to his right. Mike turned, finding Billy, whom he called over. He walked slowly, his face red and teary. Moving closer, Billy, who was followed by his adoptive mother, came to stand next to Alfred. After gazing at Billy, Rudy found Megan standing close by, flanked by her parents. Despite Rudy's sadness, he couldn't help but smile. Despite all that had happened, he recalled the relief he had felt when he wrote her discharge papers. He smiled at them, knowing that they had decided to stay close by to pay respects to their daughter's lost friend. Lastly was little Tim, who still refused to be helped by his mother, while he gave Rudy a sad wave of his hand. Betances, who had been there since before Rudy arrived, stood behind all of them in silence.

Rudy knew that not unlike him, Mike was not a practicing Catholic, but having been raised as such, he had arranged for a priest to say a few words.

After the small service, Mike came close to the casket. Forcing a smile, he nodded to the priest. Then he turned to Billy.

Rudy gazed at Billy as well, finding the boy resting against his adoptive mother. She held him tightly and tenderly. His face now flushed, he cried profusely, sighing as he attempted to catch his breath. Mike's face contorted momentarily. Rudy knew Mike fought his own heartbreak as he placed his hand on Billy's shoulder. Then Mike signaled to the two men standing beside the casket. Immediately the men opened the casket, slightly, but enough for Mike to take one last look at Maria. Rudy stood close, but not close enough to see her. He did manage to see Mike's face, which changed as he peered inside. An expression of pure anguish and heartbreak washed over Mike's face. In a heartbeat, Rudy was overcome with a thorough sadness he could ill describe.

Mike raised the plush bunny to his chest and hugged it tightly as silent tears ran down his face. His lips contorted, but he allowed no more to show. For a long moment he held onto the toy tightly, and then finally placed it inside the casket.

On instinct, Rudy moved closer. He caught one last glimpse of Maria as Mike placed the toy on her unmoving chest. He carefully moved her right arm over the bunny as if to protect it. Deeply moved, Rudy was struck by how different Maria looked. Her unmoving face was a stark contrast to the smiling girl he had known, and that made him miss her even more. Rudy then gazed up at Mike, who stood frozen, watching Maria with longing. Mike silently spoke to her, mouthing just two words, which Rudy managed to make out.

"Thank you."

Mike then moved back, and with a slight motion, signaled the cemetery staff, who dutifully closed the casket. They carefully began to lower it.

It was then that Mike's father arrived, followed by two men who looked like his security. He nodded as he walked over to Mike but said nothing. Doctor Betances, who had moved to stand close to Mike, placed his hand on Mike's shoulder and walked away, acknowledging Rudy as did. He didn't have to say anything. Rudy knew he detested Mike's father.

While the casket was lowered, Rudy again saw tears on Mike's pale face and felt his own as he struggled with his own sadness. But like Mike, Rudy didn't allow more to show. It was then that Rudy felt someone reach for his hand and hold on tightly. Surprised, he turned to find Julia, smiling sadly. She seemed to read the surprise in Rudy's expression, because she forced a smile as if to say, "I know," crying as she sighed deeply. Rudy felt her frozen hands; her thin jacket was useless in the cold weather of that dark day. Rudy took off his coat and carefully placed it over her shoulders. Crossing her arms beneath it, Julia moved closer to Rudy. Instinctively, Rudy placed his hand over her shoulder. With a teary smile, she attempted to rest her head on his shoulder. Since she was a bit taller than Rudy, the motion felt awkward, so she just stood close to him, again reaching for his hand.

With the casket now in the ground, Mike's father nodded and walked away. Mike watched him go in silence. He waited for his father to drive away before turning and addressing everyone there.

"Thank you for coming. I'm at a loss, but I'll try to do my best."

He reached inside his coat and pulled out a piece of paper, and for a second he examined it. Rudy could tell whatever was written there held great value to Rudy. Mike then forced a smile and began to speak, but he wasn't reading from the paper.

"I still marvel at Maria. Although her body was tired and failing, this little girl, who most bravely had accepted her fate, fought. That which lay inside of her, that which some might call her spirit, was so very strong and that part of her so desperately wanted to live. And she did live, what little she could. She fought hard, but in the end it was a struggle she could not win. Refusing to go gentle into the night, she did rage against the dark, even in her last moments. I do take some solace that as she wanted, she did not die alone. Around her was everyone who had cared for her those last few weeks. All the people she had touched, all the people whose lives she had made better. She certainly made mine better. Perhaps it is fitting that today is Christmas."

With that, he raised the paper in his hand.

"This is her letter to Santa. She only asked for one thing. I'm so glad I could give her in advance what she most desperately wanted: a family."

It was then that Billy, Megan, and Tim, who stood beside him, moved close to the edge and dropped flowers on Maria's casket. Watching it all, Rudy nodded silently, knowing she had made him better, and despite his profound sorrow, he was so thankful for having known her. Rudy loved her for all she unknowingly did for him, and hoped she knew they all loved her.

***

After the service, most everyone moved into Mike's home, including Julia and Rudy.

Rudy had been inside the large house before, but it always felt foreign. The paintings on the walls, the décor, and the ambience made it feel more like a seventeenth-century manor than a modern dwelling—like a museum, but cold and barren. Rudy had often wondered what it must have been like for Mike to grow up in a place like this.

After they had become friends, Rudy once asked Mike about growing up there. Mike replied, saying he hated his home, where he usually felt lonely. It was quite some time later that Mike had confided in Rudy that his fondest childhood memories came from the time he spent on the staff floor. He had often remarked that his house staff—Mike never used the term servants—felt more like his family than his father ever had.

"I don't like this place," Rudy remarked.

"Neither do I," Julia agreed.

Rudy didn't feel like eating, but he asked Julia if she wanted something anyway.

"No, you?" Julia asked.

"No," Rudy replied.

For a long time, they watched Mike from afar as he greeted the guests, taking time to talk to everyone. Lost in thought, Rudy didn't notice Megan, who walked over to him, followed by her parents close behind.

"Megan, you look great. I love your hat," Rudy said, truly glad to see the smiling girl.

"Thank you," replied Megan.

"You are welcome," replied Rudy, motioning Julia closer. "Megan, this is my friend, Julia."

Megan smiled broadly.

"I know who she is. There are some pictures of her in one of my magazines. Pleased to meet you," Megan said shyly.

"Magazines. I know, she does that a lot," Rudy said, making a face and smiling.

That made Megan smile.

"Rudy, are you okay?" Megan asked.

Surprised by the question, Rudy was unsure what to say as he was most certainly not okay, but Megan didn't wait for an answer.

"It's okay to be sad. We have to remember her, and play every day, just like she wanted," Megan said while her small hand wiped a lone tear from her still-pale face.

Rudy nodded, holding back his own tears while he admired the wise girl in front of him.

CHAPTER 30

It was a long time before Mike managed to make his way to Rudy and Julia. Noticing that Julia and Rudy held hands, Mike gazed in turn at both of them. Cocking his head, Mike summoned a difficult smile while he stretched his arms and reached for both of them. In an instant, they found themselves in a tight embrace. It was within this private huddle that Mike allowed himself to break down. Unable to do otherwise, Rudy did as well. It was more than a few minutes before Mike composed himself and emerged from the sanctuary of their small huddle. Mike straightened his clothes and gave Julia and Rudy a close look.

"This seems like a right fit," He placed his right hand on Rudy's shoulder. "Yeah, I'm glad you two found each other."

Rudy and Mike exchanged looks but didn't say anything.

Smiling again, Mike offered Rudy his hand, which Rudy took absently.

"Thank you. Thank you for being my friend when no one else would," Mike said.

"Jesus!" Rudy replied as he pulled him into a hug.

A second later, Mike hugged Julia and then turned to Doctor Betances, who, unbeknownst to Rudy, had been standing not far from them. Mike moved closer and offered him his hand. Betances reached for it, a perceptive expression on his face.

"Thank you, Doctor Betances. It was . . . it was most enlightening," Mike said.

"Thank you," replied Betances, whose tone was full of pride and not derogatory as it had been before.

"Me?" asked Mike.

"For restoring my faith in people," Betances added.

Mike reflected on what was clearly a compliment. Stunned, Mike grimaced, seeming to grasp the implication.

"It's a good thing. Be proud of it," Betances said.

Mike seemed unable to respond. He finally managed to speak, but did not address Betances's comment.

"I have to go. I have to take care of a few things."

"We'll see you later?" Rudy asked.

"Sure," Mike said, smiling before he turned.

Rudy watched Mike walk away and out of sight. Despite his assurance otherwise, Rudy had the feeling that he was not going to see Mike again.

"Have a good evening," said Betances, interrupting Rudy's contemplation. He smiled and gave a small, queer bow to Julia and silently walked away.

"Come on. We need a drink," said Julia, motioning for Rudy to follow her.

They drove to a place in Venice Beach, one Rudy had come to learn was a favorite of Julia's. There they ordered drinks and some food. The food went untouched, as did the drinks. Rudy's mind was still lost. He was distraught and he didn't have the stomach for food or drink. Regardless, he was glad he was not alone; he was most glad Julia was there.

"Rudy," Julia said.

"Yeah?" replied Rudy.

"I have to tell you something."

"What?" asked Rudy.

"Before I tell you, I want you to understand I didn't mean for any of this to happen, but I'm glad it did. You have become very important to me. Please hear me out."

Having been on the receiving end of several conversations like the one he feared was coming, Rudy decided that after all that had happened, he'd rather not go through with this conversation. Heartbroken, he reached into his pocket and placed some money on the table, enough to cover their order.

"It's okay. I'd rather not have this conversation, not today," Rudy said as he stood up, trying with all his wits to understand why she would do this on this day.

"No, wait. It's not what you think," Julia said.

Thinking he would surely come to regret his decision, Rudy turned back.

"Please sit," said a red-faced Julia.

Rudy sat, feeling a deep burning sensation in the pit of his stomach. How could she do this today of all days, he kept asking himself.

"You have to understand I didn't expect this to happen. I have to be truthful. I want to be truthful. You have to know," Julia said.

Rudy cursed himself for not having the good sense to leave earlier.

"I do like you, but . . ." Julia hesitated. "But it all began because Mike asked me to."

"What?" asked Rudy.

"I really didn't think much of you when I first met you. But Mike asked me to keep you away from the hospital, and away from him," Julia said.

"What?" Rudy asked again, confused.

"Mike didn't want you to know he was spending all that time at the hospital, so he asked me to keep you occupied. I did. I'm ashamed I did, but I didn't expect that after getting to know you, things would change. I do like you. I just want you to know the truth," Julia said.

Of all the things Rudy had been expecting to hear, this was the furthest from his mind. Julia had tricked him. It was a ruse. What little was left of his heart crumbled in disappointment. How could she do this to him? How could Mike ask her to? Rudy stood back up, frowned, and looked straight at Julia, speaking as he shook his head.

"It's not you, it's me. That would have been better."

With that, Rudy walked out of the restaurant. Julia called after him, but he was driven, angry by what he felt was a deep betrayal.

CHAPTER 31

A few days later, Rudy still felt numb. He was back in the hospital. Everyone went about their work, but it wasn't the same. It was late afternoon and Rudy had just finished afternoon rounds with Andropov. He was working on some charts at the nurses' station when Betances arrived back from dealing with the day's lone consult.

"Done?" Betances asked.

"Almost," Rudy said.

"Finish up, get your things, and meet me at my office," Betances said before walking out of the ward.

Unsure, Rudy continued his work. A few minutes later, he gathered his things. Still feeling curious about Betances's request, Rudy tried to shake off a sense of foreboding. Andropov, who seemed to have been watching him, came closer.

"I'm supposed to be on call," Rudy said.

"No, your clerkship is over. I filled out your evaluation this morning. Betances signed off on it," Andropov said, offering his hand to Rudy.

Rudy shook hands, dumbfounded.

"Doctor Dell," Andropov sneered playfully. "Rudy, it was a real pleasure working with you. I'm sure you'll do well in the future. Good luck!"

"Thank you, Doctor Andropov," Rudy replied.

"Sergio, please," Andropov replied.

"Sergio," Rudy made a production of pronouncing the name. "I thought it was Sergei."

"Sergei? I'm not Russian, I'm from Puerto Rico," Andropov said, laughing. "When you see your friend Mike, tell him it was a pleasure as well."

"It's been almost four days since I heard from him," replied Rudy. It had been as long since Rudy had talked to Julia, but he wasn't about to tell him that.

"I think it was hardest on him," Andropov said.

Rudy nodded.

"I'll see you around, Doctor," Andropov said before returning to work.

Rudy hoisted his bag over his shoulder and turned, only to find Nurse Johansson and Nurse Ramirez blocking his way. Johansson smiled, hugged him, and walked away without saying a word.

"She's weird," Ramirez said, smiling.

"That she is," Rudy said.

"Going away present," Ramirez said, and handed Rudy a small aluminum can.

Rudy accepted the gift and examined it.

"Condensed milk?" Rudy asked in confusion.

"Get some good strong coffee and add that," Ramirez said.

"Oh!" Rudy said. "I'll guard your secret."

"You better. Good luck to you, Doctor Dell," Ramirez said, turning and leaving Rudy alone with Hathaway.

"This place scars you," Hathaway said.

"I was not prepared," Rudy replied.

"No one ever is," Hathaway replied. "Never forget where you got your scars, how, or why."

"I'll try."

"You'll be a good doctor. I do hope I see you again," Hathaway said.

Rudy continued down the hallway and out of the ward, thinking that he might never again step through these doors. Rudy turned and stared long and hard at the entrance before he walked away from the oncology ward one last time, sure that a part of him would stay behind in that long hall, in those small rooms, with all those brave children.

Rudy walked up to the elevator but came to a stop when he realized that he didn't know where Betances's office was. Rudy turned back only to see Hathaway smiling back at him.

"Office eleven thirty-eight," Hathaway said.

"Thanks."

Rudy climbed into the elevator and pressed the button for the eleventh floor. After a short climb, the doors opened to a long hall of office suites. Rudy followed the numbers until he came to Betances's door. It was simply labeled with his name and the office number, no titles.

Rudy came close to the door and was about to knock when a voice called out from inside.

"Come in," Betances said.

Rudy did and walked into a small waiting room. It was the typical pediatric waiting room, with toys everywhere and a TV in a corner. On the wall opposite the entrance was the usual check-in counter, and to its side, a door. Rudy walked up and opened the door.

"Have a seat," Betances said, pointing to the chair across from his desk.

Rudy did and silently watched as Betances opened a drawer in his desk. From the low drawer he produced two small crystal shot glasses. Reaching once more into the drawer, Betances produced a bottle of whiskey. He then poured the dark, caramel-colored liquid into the glasses laid out in front of him. He pushed one of the glasses towards Rudy before he raised his glass, staring as he waited for Rudy to do the same. Rudy did and then waited for Betances, who seemed set to make a toast. He seemed to do so in silence, then after a second he raised his small glass up and frowned as he brought the glass to his mouth, drinking half of its contents. Rudy followed suit, but downed the contents of his glass in one gulp.

"Savor it. It's the good stuff!" remarked Betances while he poured a second glass for Rudy.

"Doctor Betances, how do you deal with it?" Rudy asked.

"Call me Ray," Betances replied.

Rudy nodded.

"You want to know if you get used to it? If you become detached?" Betances asked.

Rudy nodded.

"You never do, at least not if you are human. I see every face, every smile. They are always there, never far," Betances replied.

He then got up and walked up to one of the walls of his office. Like all the other walls, it was pasted with children's drawings. Some looked bright and new. Others looked worn, their colors bleached by time. Still others had but ghost images of what they once were. Betances sipped his whiskey as he carefully touched some of the drawings.

"Even without these, I could never forget about any of them," Betances said, moving his hand over the drawings. He continued until his hand found a bright drawing, which Rudy instantly recognized as Maria's.

Rudy stared openly at the drawing, his thoughts full of self-doubt.

"Will I ever be worthy?" asked Rudy.

"That is the question, isn't it?" replied Betances.

"I don't think I am."

Betances finished his drink and poured a second one.

"The world tells us to turn away, to become comfortably numb. Many do. But you, you didn't and you won't. You are like me," Betances said, placing his drink on the desk before he continued. "Never forget this glimpse. Embrace it, use it to become stronger, but don't let it consume you. Draw strength from it, and be glad you helped them as much as you could. Honor their memory by becoming a better doctor. Honor them by helping all whom you can. Honor them by being compassionate, but not weak."

His words reverberated in Rudy's mind.

"Hope I can," Rudy said, unsure.

Betances reached for his drink and swallowed it in one big gulp.

"I'll do my best," Rudy added.

"That's all we can hope to do. That's how we try to be worthy."

With a sad and forced smile, Rudy nodded.

"Rudy," Betances said, using his first name for the first time. "That you are earnest about your doubts, about measuring up to their precious gift, that is the honor they deserve. That's how you prove your worth."

Betances moved back to his desk. "Go see that girl of yours," Betances added.

Rudy's expression must have changed upon hearing the words and Betances seemed to pick up on it.

"Oh, I see," Betances said.

CHAPTER 32

A bemused Rudy walked into the elevator, pressed the button labeled "lobby," and watched as the doors closed. An uneasy feeling made him inhale slowly as the elevator began its downward movement. The doors opened earlier than he expected. Surprised, he checked to make sure he had reached the ground floor.

The last few weeks he had taken the long way around, walking out of the hospital's side exit, avoiding the emergency room all together. That meant he had to circle around the outside of the hospital to get to the staff parking, but he avoided being consulted by anyone in the emergency room. Today it was cold, and in his present state he didn't feel like making the long trek around. If he just walked across the emergency room, he would come out at its main entrance, which was right across from the staff parking. Before, he could have been stopped, consulted, but no longer. His clerkship was done. Still, the staff wouldn't know. Wanting to leave as soon as possible, he decided to chance it and walk across the emergency room.

Decisively he moved past the double doors and into the large expanse that was the emergency room. The overwhelming surprise of a few weeks ago when he had ventured through this room with Mike was no longer. The sounds and commotion were still there, but the many trips down here had come to mute the tempestuous ambience.

His gaze wandered as he moved, dodging fast-moving gurneys, nurses, and doctors. Most everyone ignored him, until he felt an attentive gaze trained upon him. Still moving, Rudy searched until coming to the eyes so interested in him. It was Doctor Zamberg. As always, she stood among a group of residents and students. Meeting Rudy's gaze, she acknowledged him with an almost imperceptible nod and a slight smile. Rudy returned the gesture as best as he could. He wondered if she knew. Her somewhat compassionate gaze confirmed it. She knew, he was sure.

Rudy continued outside and into the large parking lot. Finding his car, Rudy climbed inside it. As expected, the inside of his Jeep was cold. Unlike before, it didn't bother him as much, and the discomfort felt distant as he turned the ignition and drove away.

Rudy picked up some Chinese takeout on his way home, although he wasn't really hungry. He drove slowly, almost numb. Driving past the upscale mall, he slowed down and he found himself smiling. The memory of once running into Julia in its coffee shop was momentary, now tarnished by her betrayal. He pushed on, the lights of the city blinding until he found himself parked next to his apartment.

Upon opening his apartment door, Rudy saw a few envelopes and a small package on the floor. He stared at the small box, which the mailman had surprisingly managed to fit through the door's small mail slot. After placing the takeout on the dining table, Rudy turned back and picked up his mail, disinterestedly placing it on the table next to the takeout. He then stood looking around his small apartment, unsure of what to do next. These last few days, the work at the hospital had given him some purpose and allowed him to forget all that had happened, at least for the time being.

Now that his next clerkship wouldn't start for another week, he could study, but his mind, never mind his heart, was not in it. He couldn't call Mike; not that he hadn't tried. The times he had called, Alfred told him Mike hadn't been home since the wake. As for Julia, he wouldn't call her even if he wanted to. Not after her deception. Still unsure what to do, Rudy decided to go out and try to clear his mind. He went into his room to change. It was there that he noticed the red light on his answering machine; there was a new message. Reluctantly, he pressed the playback button.

"Hey, it's Julia. I'm so sorry, please call me. I—"

Rudy pressed the playback button, bringing the recording to a stop. He didn't want to hear the message. After a minute of cursing to himself, Rudy called his friend Pete and made plans to meet with him and a few other friends later.

Rudy walked back to his kitchen, reaching for the takeout and placing it inside the fridge so it wouldn't go to waste. It was then that the writing on the small package he had gotten in the mail caught his attention. It looked like Mike's handwriting. Picking it up for a closer inspection, Rudy scanned the script, but he didn't have to look too intently to confirm it was from Mike. The sender's address was his. Rudy opened the package to find a smaller package inside with a small card taped on it. On the card, a handwritten note read:

> *She wanted you to have this.*
> *Mike*

Rudy hesitated for a moment but opened the second package. Inside it, he found Maria's old, weathered copy of *The Little Prince*. Seeing it made him feel out of breath and profoundly sad. Rudy fell down on his couch as he held the book, which he wasn't sure he deserved. It was then that all his strength left him. Tears welling in his eyes, Rudy fought to keep from breaking down and flipped the cover open. Instinctively, he turned to the page where Billy had written his name. To his surprise, Rudy found something else written below it. The handwriting he knew well—it had been written by Maria. After a deep painful sigh, Rudy read the text aloud.

> *Thank you for being part of my family. I hope you like my book. Never forget how to be a kid.*
> *Maria*

CHAPTER 33

PRESENT DAY

"Jesus. I have known you for so long, and you never told me about that," Luz remarked.

"No one else knows. Aside from those involved," Rudy replied.

"That book in your desk, is that the one Maria gave you?" Luz asked.

Rudy sighed as he turned and looked back at his office.

"No, I always have a copy around. It helps. The gift from Maria," Rudy's voice caught when he said her name. "That one is sealed in an oxygen-free enclosure. It was one of the few things Mercedes didn't try to take during the divorce."

"But how? How did she know about Maria? You said that only those involved knew?" Luz asked.

Rudy smirked as he allowed himself an ironic laugh. Luz gazed at him, waiting for an answer, but he didn't say anything, not just yet. He was sure it would dawn on Luz at any moment.

"Mercedes Fergusson!" Luz said.

"Mercedes Fergusson," Rudy replied.

"That's when you met?" Luz asked.

"No. Well, yes, but we didn't get together until she came to work at Long Island when I was doing my fellowship. She didn't know anyone else, so . . ." Rudy replied.

Luz pursed her lips as if thinking something over.

"Ever see Julia again?" Luz asked.

"Yes and no," Rudy replied.

"Which is it?" Luz asked.

Rudy got up and walked over to his waiting room. He reached for a table filled with magazines. He fumbled through them until he found a couple of fashion magazines. He started browsing through the pages until he came to what he was looking for. Looking intently at the full-page ad, he handed the open magazine to Luz.

"Your Julia? Is that Julia?" Luz asked with great surprise.

"She's not *my* Julia," Rudy said, feeling a sting as he said the words.

"You never sought her out, not after the divorce?" Luz asked.

"No," replied Rudy with a deep sigh. "I felt betrayed by her."

"I don't think she meant to do that. I actually think that she was trying to come clean. I think she really liked you," Luz said.

"I think so now, but I didn't at the time. No use crying over spilled milk," Rudy said, knowing his expression spoke volumes more and that Luz could read him like an open book. She seemed to pick up on it and changed the subject.

"So, are going? You are, right?" Luz asked.

"I have to. I mean, I do," Rudy said.

"Of course you do," Luz said.

"Yeah," Rudy said.

Rudy stood up and wondered what Mike was up to. Why come back after all these years? Why not call him, or just show up? Why the invitation? Then he saw the clock in his waiting room. It was quite later than he thought.

"Oh, Luz, I'm sorry I kept you. You won't beat the traffic now," Rudy said.

"Are you kidding me? That story was worth it. You are always saying you want to write. Sit down and write that," Luz said as she began tapping the screen of her phone.

"I don't know," Rudy said.

"Do. Did you have any plans?" Luz asked.

"Not really," replied Rudy.

"John is close by. We won't beat the traffic. He texted saying he could meet us at that Mexican place we order lunch from. It's only a few blocks away. We can walk it," Luz said.

"Why not?" replied Rudy.

"Perfect," replied Luz as she sent John a confirmation text. "Come on."

Luz reached for her purse. They walked out and closed the office door behind them. Suddenly Luz turned to Rudy and frowned.

"I know you. You are trying to come up with an excuse not to go. Don't! Go see your friend Mike on Sunday. You need to see what comes next. I think you need it. Maybe he does too. Anyway, you have to write the next chapter."

As they stood in front of the elevator waiting, Luz turned, puzzled.

"How did you do on that test?"

"What?" Rudy asked, then, suddenly realizing what she meant, "passed by the skin of my teeth!"

Chapter 34

The hot, sunny afternoon air was a stark contrast to the cool interior of Mike's house. After all these years, the house looked different than Rudy remembered. The bleak interior colors of the past had been replaced with a more inviting palette. Unlike before, the house looked welcoming; it looked lived in. Rudy hadn't been inside for years, but he was sure it was different.

The staff directed Rudy into the large room used for gatherings. The last time he had been there had been for Maria's wake, and crossing the threshold gave him an uncomfortable sense of déjà vu. Unlike his last visit, the room looked alive with a buzz of excitement. Rudy scanned the room looking for Mike, but he couldn't find him anywhere.

"Rudy," a distant but familiar voice called. Rudy turned to see Julia a few feet behind him, looking as radiant as ever. Time seemed to have stood still for her. Rudy smiled, truly lost for words, as she came closer.

"It's been a long time," Julia said, cautiously moving closer.

"It has," Rudy said.

"Rudy, I'm truly sorry for—" Julia started, but Rudy raised his hands in a plea for her to say no more.

"Don't, you don't have to," Rudy said as he reached over and embraced Julia, who held on to him tightly.

It was quite some time before they let go of each other. When they did, Rudy gazed at her, and he was sure she returned the look. No words had to be said; it was as if that night so long ago had never happened. An older and somewhat wiser Rudy had learned to read people a little better. He could see she was truly glad to see him.

"Plastic surgeon to the stars. Bravo," Julia finally said.

"No. It's not how it sounds," Rudy replied.

"Yes it is, but you know what I like the most?"

"What?" asked Rudy.

"The work you do with underprivileged patients, especially the children. The work you do privately, the work you don't allow to be publicized," Julia said.

"How do you know about that?" Rudy asked.

"I have been keeping tabs on you," Julia replied, shrugging.

"I should have—" Rudy managed, but Julia cut him off.

Smiling, she shook her head and reached for his arm, pulling him along as she had done those many years before.

"I'm going to make it easy for you. We are having dinner," Julia said.

"I would like that," Rudy replied as he gazed into her light blue eyes, which she seemed to notice.

"Do you know what this is all about?" Julia then asked.

"No idea. I haven't seen Mike since the wake," Rudy said. "You?"

"Same, but I'm sure we'll soon find out. Let's get something to drink," Julia said.

On their way to the bar, a young man came closer to them. He wore a cheerful smile and dark gray surgical scrubs, which fit tightly, making it clear he was in good shape. He wore the messy hairstyle found on most surgeons after a day of work. The young man had an air of confidence about him. Nevertheless, he approached Rudy warily.

"Doctor Dell, it is truly great to see you. It's been so long," the young man said, extending his right hand.

Rudy shook the man's hand, trying to place him, but for the life of him he couldn't. Rudy assumed that at some point this young man had been one of his students. Having taught medical school more than ten years back East, there were far too many students for Rudy to remember all of them. Regardless, Rudy scanned the young man's face, trying to find something to spark some recollection. There was something, but even after reading his name on the scrubs, Rudy was still at a loss.

"I'm sorry, Doctor Cratchit. I'm having the hardest time placing you," Rudy said.

"Maybe this will help," Cratchit said.

Giving Rudy a knowing smirk, Cratchit reached for his pant leg, pulling it up to reveal a prosthetic limb.

"The name is Tim."

Rudy felt the wind knocked out of him. He stared at Tim, then back at the leg. For a while, that's all he could do. Holding his breath, he gazed back and forth. It was impossible. Was this that little boy that he had last seen so long ago? As if perceiving Rudy's astonishment, Tim spoke.

"I hope you still have that Roberto Clemente trading card."

"I do!" Rudy said.

Without thinking, Rudy pulled the young man into a hug, which Tim gladly reciprocated. Rudy then pushed Tim back and gazed at him.

"Let me look at you," Rudy said, now taking stock of the grown man Tim had become. Noticing the embroidery on Tim's scrubs, Rudy read them. "Doctor Cratchit, orthopedic surgeon?"

"Pediatric orthopedic surgeon. Just moved back a few weeks ago," Tim said.

"Good for you. I'm . . . I'm . . ." Rudy said, suddenly feeling unsure how to follow.

"You should be proud," Tim said. "It was you, Davenport, and Betances that inspired me to help people."

Rudy frowned. The words filled him with pride and disbelief. Not because the boy had managed to become an orthopedic surgeon; Rudy couldn't believe that at that uncertain time in his life, he was able to be such a positive influence.

"Do you still love the Yankees?" Rudy asked.

"Best team in the league. I still try to hit a few balls now and again."

Remembering Julia, Rudy introduced her, and after exchanging a few pleasantries, Tim excused himself.

"Doctor Dell, I can't stay but I would really like to catch up. Mind if I give you a call?" Tim asked.

"Rudy, call me Rudy. Not at all," Rudy said, shaking hands with him once more. After Tim left, Rudy turned to Julia.

"I need a drink."

"I bet that's quite a story," Julia said. "You can tell me all about it at dinner."

Several minutes later, while at the bar, Rudy felt someone place a hand on his shoulder. He turned in surprise to see a somewhat older and balder Mike smiling back at him. Julia reacted quickly, reaching for Mike and pulling him into a hug as soon as she realized who he was.

"Jesus," Julia managed before releasing him.

Mike smiled, gazing at both of them, again placing his hand on Rudy's shoulder.

"I'm glad you two found each other. Again," Mike said, frowning. "I'm sorry. I feel responsible for what happened between you two."

Rudy raised his hands.

"It's okay, man," Rudy said.

After a moment's hesitation, Rudy reached over and hugged Mike.

"I missed you, buddy," Mike said.

"Me too. Where the hell have you been?" Rudy asked, truly grateful to see his old friend.

"Here and there and everywhere. It's a long story," Mike said as he looked in turn at Julia and then at Rudy. "You know, you two are my best friends," Mike said.

"Then why so long?" Rudy asked.

"There's no easy way to explain, so I won't. I did keep tabs on you, on both of you," Mike said as he considered his next words. "I still feel that what happened between you two is my fault."

"We are having dinner tonight. We'll take it from there," Julia said.

"You can't have dinner tonight, well, at least not by yourselves," Mike said, shaking his head.

"Why not?" Julia asked.

"Come on, I want you to meet someone. I'll explain then," Mike said as he pointed to a far corner of the large room.

With mild reluctance, Julia and Rudy headed in the direction Mike pointed. Julia walked a few steps in front of Rudy, with Mike behind them pointing the way.

"It's just right through there," Mike said, pointing to the door leading to the main kitchen. Julia nodded, pushing the door open. It was then that Mike reached for Rudy's arm, holding him tightly so that he came to an abrupt stop.

"Don't let her go, not this time."

With that, Mike let Rudy go and again pointed to the large kitchen doors. Rudy pushed the door open and Mike moved ahead, asking Rudy to follow him. Inside they found a confused Julia waiting. Mike pointed to a far door on the left, which Rudy recognized immediately. It led to Alfred's apartment. The group headed in, and there on the floor was Alfred, playing with a small girl. She wore a formal gown, which was becoming a mess. Beside them was a beautiful, slender woman with exotic features, olive skin, and large expressive brown eyes. She smiled when she saw Mike.

"Is this Julia and Rudy?" she asked.

"Yes," Mike said, turning to his friends. "I would like you to meet Doctor Laila Kausar, my wife."

Julia smiled and reached for the woman, hugging her tightly.

"So very glad to meet you," Julia said before pursuing a fast-paced interrogation of the poor woman.

Rudy listening as Julia learned that Laila was originally from Pakistan. She grew up in London, where she went to medical school. Then she explained that while in the Peace Corps, she came across Mike. Rudy didn't catch much of the exchange after that, as Alfred stood up, straightened his tux, and walked up to him.

"How are you, Doctor Dell? It is a genuine pleasure to see you," Alfred said when Rudy interrupted him.

"Don't you dare call me that! It's very good to see you too," Rudy said as they shook hands vigorously.

"Likewise," Alfred replied.

"Do you know what this is all about?" Rudy asked him.

"There's a gathering for the stockbrokers and executives of Mister Davenport's business, preparations for a forthcoming announcement, but I'm not at liberty to discuss anything else," Alfred replied.

"No, I mean us here?" Rudy inquired.

"Leave the man alone," Mike said.

"What's going on?" Rudy asked.

"In a minute. Come meet Laila," Mike insisted.

Laila came close, smiling brightly, and hugged Rudy.

"I'm so glad to finally meet you. I have heard so much about you. Thank you for taking care of him during school," Laila said in a posh British accent.

"Mike didn't need anyone to take care of him," Rudy said, remembering that Mike had been one of the most self-reliant people he had ever met.

As if she had read his mind, she added, "Believe me, he needed it. You were and still are his friend, and he needed that the most," Laila said, eyeing Rudy and then Julia before speaking again. "Mike, you are right. They do make a good couple. They fit."

The frank remark surprised Rudy, who turned to Julia, who just smiled and shrugged.

"What's this all about?" Rudy asked.

"The gathering is one last hurrah for the board and executives. As of Monday, I'll own sixty-three percent of the company stock. From now on, things will change for the better. It's not like they'll be out of a job, but . . . Forget it. That's not why you two are here," Mike said as he motioned the little girl who had been playing with Alfred over. She moved closer and joined them.

"My wife and I would be honored if you two would accept the burden of being godparents to our daughter. The christening is next Sunday. We hope you will accept," Mike said.

"We will be honored," Julia said with excitement.

"Of course." Rudy nodded.

The little girl moved closer to Julia, smiling broadly.

"Are you my Aunt Julia and Uncle Rudy?" she asked, her accent identical to her mother's.

Julia and Rudy both nodded.

"Yes, we are," Rudy replied.

"Is it true you ran down a hall in medical school in nothing but underwear?" she asked Rudy playfully.

"Yes," Rudy replied, mortified. "Did your father tell you why?"

"He said you did it on a dare," she added with a smile.

Rudy glared at Mike, who shrugged.

"Yes, story time with Mike is best not left unsupervised. I'm dreadfully sorry," Laila said.

"It's fine. One of my proudest moments," Rudy said as he placed his hand so the little girl could high-five it, which she immediately did.

"Wait," Rudy said, suddenly realizing he didn't know the girl's name. "What's your name?"

The little girl smiled and walked back to her parents, but did not reply. Mike frowned, looking down at his daughter and then back at Rudy.

"Julia, Rudy, meet Maria."

The end.

ACKNOWLEDGEMENTS

As before I want to thank my family for their patience. That you allow me to steal time away from you, in order to write is a gift I will never be able to repay. To my beta readers, Hilda, Janice and Ana, who read the whole thing in one day, thank you!

ABOUT THE COVER ART

The illustration on the cover is an original watercolor made by my oldest daughter Natalia, and came about in a most unexpected way. I did not ask her to paint it for this work, on the contrary the painting helped the book take shape.

I was in the process of writing the first draft of *Chasing Rabbits*, it had a different name then, and I was still ironing out the kinks, the story was there, but there was something missing. Then one night I saw Natalia's painting and everything changed.

It was close to the end of the year, Natalia and her classmates had an art exhibition of sorts. The parents were invited and each student would present their works, choosing one as their favorite and explain its meaning, or rather the inspiration behind it.

Natalia chose her watercolor, the one you can see in the cover, and showed it to us as her favorite. It immediately struck me, but it was Natalia's inspiration that lit a spark inside me. In a few days time that which I felt was missing from the story came to be.

That your children inspire you may be an overused cliché, but in this case it is true.

ABOUT THE AUTHOR

Rodolfo Del Toro, is a physician with over twenty-years of experience. He has spent most of his professional life in private practice and teaching at Medical Schools, which he finds tremendously rewarding. Outside work, he enjoys traveling and spending time with his family. When he can, he steals time to write and feed, what his wife believes, is an unhealthy obsession with old Land Rovers D90s and electric guitars.

This is his second published book.

You can follow him on Instagram #del_356

Made in the USA
Monee, IL
07 September 2022

13433055R00125